NEVER LOOK
BACK

NEVER LOOK BACK

Dan Latus

ROBERT HALE · LONDON

© Dan Latus 2008
First published in Great Britain 2008

ISBN 978-0-7090-8710-6

Robert Hale Limited
Clerkenwell House
Clerkenwell Green
London EC1R 0HT

www.halebooks.com

2 4 6 8 10 9 7 5 3 1

Typeset in 10/14½pt Sabon
by Derek Doyle & Associates, Shaw Heath
Printed and bound in Great Britain
by Biddles Limited, King's Lynn

CHAPTER ONE

Today he was uneasy, on edge. He'd woken early, just before first light, and the feeling had hit him instantly. It wasn't the first time either. It had been like this, off and on, since Majorca.

He completed a tour of the cottage and returned to the spare bedroom, taking binoculars with him. As he focussed the glasses and swept the hillside, he acknowledged that it wasn't much to go on, this gut feeling. Probably nothing at all. But he couldn't ignore it, the sense that something was different, not quite right. Not since that business in Majorca.

The cottage was located just below the scarp edge on the western side of the moor, giving a distant view of the Cheviot Hills. In front, the ground fell away gently in a long, undulating swathe to the valley. Behind, to the east, a hundred yards of steep hillside swept up to the escarpment. He concentrated on that, the high ground.

The binoculars didn't reveal anything. He lowered them and stepped back. If an attack ever did come, though, this was where it would come from. The high ground to the east. He stretched and wiggled his neck and shoulders. Then he studied the hillside some more.

He'd been there for nearly three years, and there had been other occasions when he'd felt vaguely threatened by something he couldn't see. Was it paranoia? Perhaps.

Maybe he just ought to accept it, and get used to it? Maybe the feeling went with the territory. His territory.

Especially since Majorca, though it was hard to accept this. Something was happening. It wasn't all imagination.

Standing well back from the window, he scanned the hillside again. His eyes lingered on the copse of birch at the edge of the disused quarry just below the escarpment. Nothing. He could see nothing that shouldn't be there.

He gnawed his lip. He wasn't satisfied, or reassured. He lowered the binoculars and stood quite still in silent contemplation. The light was stronger now. He could see into the shadows beneath the sandstone outcrop on the skyline. But he couldn't see anything significant, anything different.

Yet something had drawn him to this window. And now it held him here. What was it?

He was slow getting there, but when he grasped the difference it hit him like a spring squall. The sheep! Where were they?

He scanned the hillside until he found them, way over to the left and much lower down than usual. Well out of position. Heads up and unsettled.

He frowned and moved to the side of the window, instinctively presenting less of a target.

He studied the sheep. Something had disturbed them and upset their rhythm. They were stolid, reliable creatures of habit, the sheep on this moor. And they were hefted, born of generations that had lived and died on this hillside and knew no other. It was their ancestral home. They worked their way around it in a daily cycle, always to be found in the same place at a given time of day. First thing in the morning they were always up high, facing east, waiting for the sun to rise above the horizon.

But today, they weren't.

So the sheep were out of position? Something had disturbed them? What of it?

It might mean something, or it might mean nothing. Nothing, probably. But there was no way of knowing so long as he remained here. He needed to get outside and have a look.

The air was cool when he opened the door and slipped out into the yard at the back of the cottage – September. No frost yet, but it wouldn't be long coming. Already the bracken on the hillside was yellowing fast, as the nights cooled and the days shortened. He gave an involuntary shiver and paused to zip up his jacket before setting off.

He didn't get far. Halfway across the yard, in the shelter of the old stone outhouse, he paused and thought about going back for the shotgun. No. He couldn't be bothered. It wasn't worth it. Now he was outside, he was already feeling less anxious; this would probably be another false alarm.

But he did go back. He wanted the Leatherman, his multi-tool knife. Sometimes sheep got themselves caught up in old wire. Things happened. It was as well to have something useful with you. Besides, Apache, the black cat that lived with him had appeared, and was standing at the back door waiting to be let in.

As he opened the door, he glanced back before he stepped inside. The light was good now. Soon the sun would be up. Even without it, the cloud-free sky promised a bright morning, and a brilliant day to follow. No wind either. Perfect.

He stooped to smooth Apache's ears and then stepped across to the dresser to reach for his Leatherman.

Given the conditions, the near perfect conditions, the first bullet shouldn't have missed. But it did.

It thudded into the wall on the far side of the kitchen, shattering the plaster and filling the air with dust and fragments of stone. Others followed before he could blink. A crater appeared. A heart-beat later the glass in the window facing the hillside disintegrated. Apache screamed and fled.

By then, Jake was on the floor, scrabbling for the shelter of the wall beneath the shattered window.

For a moment he lay still, stunned, heart racing. Then instinct and experience took over. Two bullets? He glanced at the wall. Three, probably. Maybe four. Well-grouped. Good shooting. But not good enough.

He was shaken, badly shaken, but he knew he had to get his brain in gear. And control his breathing. He was panting as if he had just sprinted through a minefield.

Concentrate! Assess and take action. The old formula.

He risked a quick glance over the sill of the broken window. There was no-one in sight. It had been long-range shooting. Whoever had done it would be cursing at having missed. The element of surprise was gone now.

He eyed the door leading out of the kitchen to the rest of the cottage. It was a long way away but he needed to reach it. Whether he went upstairs for the shotgun or not, he had to get through that doorway, and fast. Whoever was doing the shooting could be approaching the window right now, looking to finish the job.

He took the decision. He crawled to the side of the window and stood up. He braced against the wall for a moment and then hurled himself across the kitchen and through the doorway. Chunks of plaster and fragments of stone showered him but no bullets hit. He was through the gap.

The shotgun was kept in a locked case inside a locked cupboard in the bedroom he normally used. He reached the cupboard, inserted the key and unlocked it. He grabbed the shotgun and a box of shells. Immediately he felt better.

He slipped out of the front door, cut across the patch of rough grass and dived into the cover of waist-high bracken. He took a moment to catch his breath. Then he began working his way rapidly across the hillside, using the hollows and small ravines, heading uphill at speed. Only one thing on his mind now. Get there and get the bastard!

One man, he reckoned: a lone sniper.

Surprising it hadn't been a bomb. It would have been simpler. Anybody could have planted a bomb, but a sniper, a proper one at least, was a rare and valuable weapon.

Not that it mattered. There'd be time to work out later what was happening, and who it was. If he had an opportunity to think it through there would be plenty of possibilities to choose from.

He kept an eye out for movement – no sign of anyone approaching the cottage. Either the sniper was waiting for him to show himself again or he'd quit and gone. One man. He hoped he was still there.

Just short of the overgrown track he stopped, in cover, and kept still for a few moments. Listening. Watching.

Uphill from the cottage, the track led to the old quarry. He was pretty sure it was the quarry where the shots had come from. So whoever had gone up there might now be making his way back down the track. Worth waiting for him.

It wasn't. After a couple of minutes he decided it wasn't going to happen. He pushed on.

The high bracken gave way to low heather. He paused before he broke cover to scan the escarpment and what he could see of the quarry. From here on he would be very exposed if he took the direct route. But was anyone there still? Maybe not.

He began to get to his feet and almost immediately felt and heard the air vibrate. The bullet missed. He threw himself back down, cursing. Someone was still there. And someone now knew where he was.

More cautiously, he took the long route round, using the bracken as cover, he got as close as he could. He reached the boulders and slabs of rock at the entrance to the quarry and peered gingerly around them. He couldn't see anyone. He skirted all around the edge. Nothing. No sign of anyone. It was the same on top of the escarpment. If someone was still around, they were well dug in.

He stood still and let his eyes roam, looking for something, anything, that shouldn't be there. Then he heard what sounded like a motor bike engine coughing into life. He wheeled round and stared across the moor to the north. Moments later a quad bike sped into view, bouncing wildly across the rough ground on its balloon tyres. Already it was half a mile away. One man on it.

He nodded. So that was how it was done. He'd come over the moor. Probably had a bigger vehicle parked somewhere over there. Somewhere near Haddon Wood, maybe, a mile and a half away.

He grimaced with frustration and spent futile moments staring into the distance. Then he dropped down into the quarry and began hunting around. He knew for certain now that that was where the sniper had been located, but he found nothing. No shell cases or bits of paper, or anything else. Still less the impression of a body on the ground. Nothing.

He stood gazing down at the cottage. Two hundred yards to two-fifty, at the outside. Pretty good shooting, considering the circumstances. The distance wasn't anything special and the light was reasonable. But the guy hadn't had much to aim at, shooting through glass into an unlit interior. Hardly anything at all, in fact.

He could have got closer, and made sure, but he'd probably been waiting for him to come outside into the open. That's what he'd have done. Waited.

Then, when the target had turned back into the cottage, he'd had a go anyway. Maybe he'd got fed up with waiting. Maybe he was cold. Or pushed for time.

Not a top-class sniper, then. A really good one would wait all day and night long if necessary – in snow or rain, sub-zero temperatures, whatever – and still make the hit when the time came, as it always did if you waited long enough. This had been just a guy, though. Just a guy who'd fancied his chances, and he'd messed it up. He'd missed.

Jake shrugged and set off downhill back to the cottage. He'd been lucky. The sniper should have waited longer. Not that it mattered now what he had or hadn't done.

As for the 'who' . . . Lots of possibilities, he thought grimly, after all his years in the service. Finding him wouldn't have been easy, but he'd always known one day someone would take the trouble to do it. That day seemed to have arrived.

CHAPTER TWO

At mid-morning Jake went into the village, taking the old Land Rover. It was two miles on the rough track from the cottage, and then another mile-and-a-half on pot-holed tarmac. He saw no-one on the way, just sheep, and some rooks out scavenging.

Most of his stuff was in the Land Rover. What he thought worth keeping. What he wouldn't want to lose.

Plus Apache, who hadn't wanted to go but couldn't just be left. Jake wasn't confident Apache had it in him to become a genuine wildcat.

As for himself, he didn't know what he was going to do yet. He'd been found though. So one possibility was not returning to the cottage. Ever. He was ready for that.

Another possibility was going back anyway. Ignoring the morning's events. It all depended. As much as anything, it depended on whether the man – or woman – with the rifle was going to stick around and try again. Jake rather hoped he or she would. It would give him a chance to sort it out. That would be better than having to worry and look over his shoulder for ever more.

The village was called Cragley. It was not very big and it was quiet, especially now, on a Thursday morning. The weekend was near but the summer holidays were over. Schools had been back in session for a couple of weeks now and not many visitors were left in this part of Northumberland.

He bought a newspaper and sat on a bench on the village green with it. He turned the pages occasionally without reading them. He wanted to think things through, and to see what, if anything, was going on in the village. Not much, it seemed.

Although no sooner had he thought that than an ambulance and a police car sped past, lights flashing on both of them. They didn't stop anywhere in the village. Heads turned with their passing, but people soon got back to what they had been doing before.

Normal life resumed; shopping at the little Co-op supermarket and the smell of new bread and hot Aberdeen Angus beef pies from the home bakery. A succession of beat-up old Land Rovers and pickups at the diesel pump in front of the garage. The landlord from The King's Arms opened his front door, stood at the top of the steps and raised a glass invitingly. Jake grimaced and shook his head.

Back to normal, then. Reassuringly normal. No mad gunman opening up with a machinegun. No suicide bombs. Nothing. It was as if the morning's events had all been a bad dream.

So maybe he would stay. He'd weathered worse situations than this. If they came for him again he would just have to handle it.

After all, he liked it here. Or he had until now, until this morning.

He took a fresh look around – old stone houses in the thin sunlight; ancient church, and a chapel; three pubs; a few shops. Giant horse-chestnut trees and sycamores stood around the green, rustling in a faint breeze. The scent of fresh-cut grass from the churchyard. Elderly people shuffling along the pavement, entering the tea-shop, or coming out of the bank or the hairdresser's. A woman with two toddlers and a baby in a pram laboured up the slope from Town Foot.

Normality.

Except somebody had just tried to kill him.

He studied the passing faces, hoping to find a clue. Most of the people he'd seen before often enough. He nodded to the postman sorting through the envelopes in his hand, and got a greeting back in return. He smiled and turned to look across the green.

He watched a tall, blonde young woman meandering along the pavement. A visitor he guessed – nice looking; never been here before by the way she was gazing all around her with such obvious fascination, clearly interested in everything she could see.

Surprisingly, she didn't spend long gazing in the window of the famous shoe shop that attracted people from miles around. And she had only a cursory glance at the posh frock shop. Interested more in the window above the chemist's. And, inevitably, in the estate agent's window. Everyone visiting Cragley looked to see if there were any bargains on the housing front, which there weren't, of course. Not any more. Every ruined hovel and collapsing cow shed in the district had long since been snapped up.

The blonde woman really was having a good look round. On her own, too. No sign of a companion. Surprising for someone with her looks. She wore tight black trousers, a cream t-shirt and a light-weight, bright orange, outdoor jacket. Great breasts, from what he could see. She had a smile for every passer-by, even one for Jake when he caught her eye.

He smiled back and wondered if she was American. Then he wondered why she was so interested in the buildings above ground-floor level, like the window above the chemist's. She could be flat hunting, he supposed. Or she could be a student of vernacular architecture, interested in the mouldings around the windows or the patterns in the stonework.

Somehow, though, he didn't think so. Unlikely though it seemed, the more he studied her, the more he began to think she had an interest, a professional interest. And that interested him. Quite a lot, in fact. Especially today.

It was her first visit. Others had been before, but she hadn't. She thought the village pleasant enough in its rather austere way. Quiet and slow, perhaps, but unblemished by modern development.

More to the point, there shouldn't be any difficulty here – which was probably why they'd sent her. Good experience. No real problems. What was it Ed had said, in his old-fashioned, affected language? Piece of cake! She smiled at the recollection.

Then she compiled a mental inventory of risk factors: a wide, open street with clear sight lines and plenty of cover from parked vehicles. She glanced at the first-floor of the buildings on the far side of the road. The same as this side. Lots of windows, all of them with a good view of the main street and everything in it. She particularly liked the stone balcony and accompanying balustrade above the ancient bank building. It was big enough to house an artillery unit! Not that anyone would dare use it, of course – far too obvious.

And people were so courteous and trusting here. That was a worry. They made eye contact and smiled. Many even spoke. Good morning, good morning! How are you today? The friendliness would make it easier. It meant people would be less wary. That was something to point out.

She watched the ambulance and police car speed past, lights flashing. That was something else she needed to check: travel time to the nearest hospital.

Not that there should be any need, probably. And even if there was, they'd use the helicopter. They wouldn't go by road. Unless . . . unless the chopper wasn't big enough for all the casualties, or there was a mechanical failure, or something worse. A hit, maybe. A heat-seeking missile.

Not here, surely! She gave a little grimace, but you had to allow for these possibilities: all possible contingencies, they had told her.

She stood at the top of the street – what did they call it? 'Main Street'? Cute! – and gazed down its length one last time. She'd seen enough. For now. She would get back and study the maps and plans now that she had a better feel for the place. Then she would let them know, give them her advice, her professional opinion. See how they liked it. Not much, probably.

She was under no illusions. The older guys didn't like her, couldn't be bothered with her. Thought she was a waste of space. The young ones didn't think that, of course, but they didn't count. Anyway, she knew why most of them liked her. Randy bunch! She smiled ruefully.

The man sitting on the bench beneath the horse-chestnut tree was another one. He wasn't all that young, but he kept studying her. You would have thought he'd seen enough by now. She gave him a sunny smile and turned away.

The phone in her pocket buzzed and vibrated.

'Yes?'

She listened to what he said and then replied. 'I saw the ambulance and the police car. But nothing's going on here. Nothing's happening at all.'

She continued to listen. 'Right. One body. I've got that.'

It wasn't great, she thought afterwards. Probably no linkage. All the same . . . she would stick around a while longer. She needed to know for sure. It was the sort of thing that could make a difference.

Jake called in at The Gallery to see Cedric and Caitlin.

Caitlin was wielding a feather duster, reaching into dark corners of the shop and standing on tip-toe to destroy cobwebs dangling from the ceiling. She didn't immediately look round when the door bell clanged.

'Spring won't be here for a while yet,' he said. 'You're ahead of yourself.'

'Jake!'

Caitlin spun round and laughed. 'Where did you come from? And who's that with you?'

'Apache. You remember him, don't you?'

He tickled the cat's ears. Apache decided he wanted to be on firm ground. Jake released him and he took off into a dark corner, where the clutter of antiques was at its most dense.

'He can smell the mice,' Caitlin said. 'Lord knows, we've got plenty of them here. And dust,' she added, stooping to blow some off the head of a black-marble Venus.

'You could try selling a few things,' Jake suggested, glancing around the crowded interior. 'Then you wouldn't have so much dusting to do.'

'Sell things? Oh, no! That wouldn't do. Not at all. We'd have nothing for customers to look at then.'

'Just a few things, I meant. Just enough for customers to be able to get inside the shop.'

'What a cynical man you are, Jake.'

He grinned. He knew she didn't mean it. In fact, he knew she liked him a lot. And he liked her in return. If only she'd been twenty years younger, and not married to Cedric, who knew what might have happened?

'You don't mind cats?' he asked.

She shook her head. 'Not ones like Apache.'

'Can I leave him with you for a while?'

'Why? Are you going away?'

He hesitated. 'Maybe. I mean, yes. Just for a while. Probably.'

'You don't seem very sure.'

'No, I'm not.'

She studied him, looking concerned. 'Jake, is everything all right?'

'Yes.' He shrugged. 'It's complicated.'

She studied him a moment longer and then said, 'Leave Apache here. We'll look after him.'

'He can look after himself,' Jake said with a small laugh. 'He usually does. But. . . .'

'You don't have to explain, Jake. And don't worry. Rupert won't eat him!'

'It's Rupert I'm worried about. Apache likes dog for dinner.'

He was relieved. He hadn't liked the idea of Apache just hanging around the cottage, waiting for someone who might never return. And he couldn't take Apache with him. He didn't know where he was going, for one thing – or even if he was going anywhere at all.

'How's business?'

'Could be better. But Cedric's pots continue to sell, even if my pictures don't.'

He was a potter, she a painter. But the antiques and old tat seemed to give them the greater part of their livelihood.

'What?' Jake said now. 'Those coffee mugs of his, the ones with Sharon and Tracy on the side? And Lee and Wayne? People actually buy them?'

'Unfair, isn't it?'

'I'd much rather have one of your paintings.'

She smiled. 'That's very sweet of you, Jake. But you can't afford my paintings.'

'When my boat comes in—'

'Is that coffee ready?' a voice called from a back room.

Caitlin looked indignant. 'Not unless you've made it!'

Jake smiled, even more so when Cedric came into view, looking slightly more dishevelled than usual. He patted himself down and was enveloped in clouds of white powder. Jake guessed he'd been potting.

'Not in here!' Caitlin shrieked. 'I've just finished dusting.'

'Sorry.' Cedric looked contrite for a moment. Then he winked and chuckled. 'Hello, Jake! Thought I heard your voice. What's going on?'

'Not much. But I'm loaning you my cat.'

'Nice.' Cedric peered around myopically. 'Not that Apache thing?'

'That's the one.'

Cedric looked unsure.

'He's a good mouser,' Caitlin said.

'Ah!' Cedric beamed. 'Just what we need. Coffee, Jake?'

'Not just now, thanks. I've got to get on.'

'Well, we'll take care of him. Where is he?'

'Getting down to work, I think.'

'He's down in the cellar,' Caitlin said. 'Already!'

Jake grinned and left them to it. Apache was one thing less for him to worry about.

CHAPTER THREE

'We got one of them.'

'But not the other, I understand?'

'Well, we got one.'

'We needed both.'

'Yeah.'

'And you were supposed to do it quietly. What happened?'

'With Sanderson?'

'Yes. With Sanderson.'

'Someone came along too soon. The farmer. We couldn't get the body away in time.'

'You couldn't divert his attention?'

'Not enough time. Either we did what we did or he saw what had happened to Sanderson. We took the decision.'

Sigh, followed by a silence.

'What about Ord?'

'I didn't get him.'

'I know that. You missed?'

'I missed.'

Long pause. Then: 'You'd better try again.'

'Right.'

'Take Grady with you.'

'Grady?'

'Don't argue.'

'I'm not arguing! I just. . . .'

'Take him.'

Silence.

'And another thing. Don't call me on this number again. I don't want to risk anyone checking the records.'

'Right. About Ord. How long have we got?'

'Six days now.'

'It's not long. We should have taken him out in Majorca.'

'We tried. Remember?'

'You should have sent me. It's not so easy here.'

'Never mind that. Just do it!'

CHAPTER FOUR

Jake wondered about the woman. What she was doing in Cragley? It might just be some sort of survey. Property values, say, or to do with council tax, but if it was, he was suspicious about her doing it here today, the day someone had taken a crack at him. Or was he being paranoid again?

It could be coincidence, but he didn't really believe in coincidence. What had kept him alive so far was the belief that things happened for a reason. If you could work out the reason, you could do a lot to protect yourself – and stay alive.

Anyway, he didn't like what had happened that morning, and he couldn't make his mind up what to do. He'd come here three years' ago to get his life back, hoping there was something left of it. He'd done that, but now it was in jeopardy again, and he wasn't sure what to do about it.

He still had the option of getting back in the Land Rover, starting the engine and moving on. Disappearing again. It was an option with a lot of appeal. Maybe he would. Just because he hadn't done it yet didn't mean he wasn't going to.

He saw Will Taylor coming along the street and got out to have a word with him. Sergeant Will Taylor, the greater part of the local constabulary, was grim-faced, different altogether to the man he occasionally had a chat with over a pint in the pub.

'Can't stop now!' Will snapped.

'What's up?'

Will grimaced. And did stop. He turned towards Jake. In a low voice, he said, 'Accident, over at Fellside Farm. The cottage there.'

'Accident?'

'Fire. One bloke dead, apparently.'

'Who is it?'

Will shook his head. 'Never met him myself. Incomer. Been there a year or two, they say, but to my knowledge I've never even seen him.'

While Jake was deliberating over whether to say anything about his own problem, which would have meant breaking cover, Will nodded and said, 'I'd better get on. See you later.'

Jake nodded and turned away. Another apparent coincidence, he thought. It was turning out to be quite a day for coincidences in Cragley.

He began to relax. The sun was shining. It was warm. Late September, a perfect time of year. He started up the Land Rover and headed back to the cottage. Carefully.

The kitchen was a mess. He swept up the bits of plaster and lath from the wall, along with chunks of stone. He gathered the fragments of glass and splintered wood from the window; some cups and plates had some-how managed to get broken too. He swept them up, as well. After some half-hearted dusting, there was plaster dust everywhere. He stared at the hole in the wall. Then, to keep out the wind and rain, he pinned a sheet of polythene over the gap where the window used to be. After that he was stuck for something to do.

He went upstairs and replaced the shotgun in its cabinet. Then he took it out again. Stupid thing to do. What made him suppose he didn't need it any more? Denial, probably, wishful thinking. But this thing wasn't over. It had hardly even started. The shotgun would stay where he could reach it.

He looked in to the room he used as a studio and gazed at all the stuff he hadn't taken with him in the Land Rover: paintings, sketches and photographs. They were of insects, mostly. And some birds. Life on the moor.

Much as he liked doing the art work, and as interesting as he'd found it, he hadn't taken it with him that morning. He hadn't put it in the Land Rover. He wouldn't now either. If he travelled, he would travel light. So it couldn't mean that much to him.

What did? Nothing much, he thought bleakly. Not since Ellie. That was the truth of it.

He left the studio and slammed the door behind him.

He spent some more time thinking through what had happened. He didn't get far. He didn't know much. Someone had had a pop at him, and he didn't know who.

After all his years in the service, he didn't even know where to start looking. Virtually all that time had been spent overseas in distant places. How likely was it that someone from the old days could have found him here, given the steps he'd taken to conceal his trail? Not very, he concluded.

His thoughts returned to the woman in the village, the stranger, the visitor. The coincidence of it. She worried him. So he'd better check her out.

She was in The Wild Orchid Room, an old-fashioned tea-shop that somehow managed to stay in business against all the odds.

He sat at an empty table and spread out a weekly newspaper he'd picked up from the shelf near the door. *The* local newspaper. A waitress he knew arrived to take his order. Tea and a fruit scone? That would do nicely, thank you.

'This is last week's paper,' he pointed out.

'How can you tell?' the waitress asked.

'From the date.' He showed her. 'Right there. It says.'

'Well, this week's is no different,' she assured him. 'I wouldn't worry you're missing anything.'

He smiled at her. 'You're not very busy?'

'We have been. It's just quiet at the minute.'

She bustled away. He directed his smile at the young woman a couple of tables away. 'On holiday?' he asked.

She stared at him coolly for a moment. 'No,' she said.

'Just visiting?'

'Just visiting,' she agreed, looking away.

She didn't want to talk. Not to him anyway. He wasn't bothered. He'd already established something he'd been wondering about. She was definitely English. And if she really was just visiting, she was visiting with a purpose. He'd seen her checking out the main street.

'This is a nice time of year to be visiting,' he suggested, turning his attention to the tea that was about to arrive.

'Yes?' the woman said vaguely.

She gathered her bits and pieces together while he poured his tea. She placed a bank note on the table and moved the sugar bowl to hold it down. She was leaving.

She gave him a faint smile as she passed by. A farewell smile. He nodded and leaned forward over the newspaper. He didn't look round when the door-bell clanged as she left.

'Now there's only you,' the waitress said, as she began to clear the adjacent table.

'Don't worry, Sylvia. I'll not be long.'

'Oh, stay – please! We don't want the place to look totally empty.'

'She was a visitor, that woman,' he suggested carefully. 'So there're one or two around still.'

'One or two. That's about all.'

'Did she say where she's from?'

Sylvia shook her head. 'Not to me, she didn't. At first I wondered if she was a reporter, but she didn't ask any questions.'

'Reporter? Why would one of them come here?'

'Well, he used to come in quite often. He would sit at that table in the corner, there, and do the crossword in the *Telegraph*.'

'Who would?'

'Him!' She sighed and added, 'That man that died in the fire. Nice man, he seemed. Quiet, like.'

Jake stared at her.

'The fire over at Fellside Farm,' she said patiently. 'Last night.'

He nodded. 'Oh, that one,' he said at last.

CHAPTER FIVE

He caught up with the tall, blonde, young woman again in The King's Arms. He'd guessed she might be there – the only hotel in the village. She was studying her mobile. Then she started to text, jabbing her index finger hard at the key pad.

She was expecting a bar meal, judging by the place setting at her table. Jake remembered he'd eaten nothing all day himself.

'Do you want to see the menu?' Tom Fairbrother, the landlord, asked.

'Has it changed?'

'Not since last year.'

'That's what I thought,' Jake said with a grin. 'I'll just have the Famous Northumbrian Sausage then.'

'A wise choice.'

'Let's hope so,' Jake said, lifting his glass.

He looked round again. The pub was quiet. It was still early evening – not many visitors; just the one, in fact, not counting himself. She was still texting with great concentration; reassuring a boyfriend or husband, perhaps. Or boss. They would take some reassuring, the way she looked. They would be worried to death when she was out of their sight.

He wondered if he was wasting his time, hanging on to her. Probably. He didn't suppose for one moment she was the one who'd taken a pot at him that morning.

He turned back to his host. 'What have you heard about that fire, Tom?'

The other man pursed his lips and continued drying glasses. 'Fellside Farm?' he said after a moment. 'The bloke that died?'

Jake nodded.

'Not a lot. It seems to have been a bad business, though.'

Jake nodded again, and waited.

'What I heard was there was no need to take what was left to the hospital.' Tom shook his head. 'The lads from the Fire Service were pretty upset when they came in here.'

They were part-timers, Jake thought, volunteers. Road-accident attenders more than firemen, shopkeepers, butcher, mechanic, joiners. They would have come in for a well-earned drink after the job was finished. He could imagine them being gutted.

'I let them have a couple of rounds on the house,' Tom added quietly. 'After what they'd had to do, they deserved it.'

There was no denying that.

'So the whole house was gone?' Jake asked.

'The cottage, you mean? No, that was all right. It was the vehicle. That's what he was found in. A big Toyota Land Cruiser, or something.' Tom shrugged. 'One of them 4-by-4s. Anyway, I can't see the point of them myself. What's wrong with a Land Rover?'

'Nothing. Nothing at all. So what happened?'

'Hard to say.' Tom shook his head. 'It was burned out. Right by the side of the track.'

Jake found that interesting. Big, expensive, modern vehicles didn't suddenly burst into flames. Not often, anyway.

'He'd crashed, had he?'

'Well . . . I don't rightly know. The Sergeant just said the vehicle was off the track leading up to the farm.'

Not a high-speed crash, then. You'd be lucky to get out of second gear on most farm tracks.

'Anyone else involved?'

'Just him, I believe.'

Jake nodded. In the mirror behind the bar he noticed the young, blonde woman was taking an interest. She was staring at them. Nothing like a disaster to tear people away from their mobiles and laptops.

'Did you know him, Tom?'

'Not really. I remember seeing him, though. He came in here once or twice. But that was about all. Nice enough fellow. Quiet, like. Pleasant. Kept himself to himself.'

'Not local?'

Tom shook his head. 'Definitely not.'

Maisie came through from the kitchen just then, carrying Jake's meal, fresh and blistered from the microwave. 'Where are you sitting?' she called.

'It doesn't matter,' he told her. 'Anywhere.'

He followed her. She put the tray down on a table close to the only other one occupied by a diner. That was fine by him. He was close to the woman without having arranged it himself. She would know he hadn't chosen the table.

He smiled and nodded at her when Maisie went off to find some cutlery for him. 'Hello, again!' he said cheerfully.

'Hi.'

She didn't seem thrilled to see him. He busied himself with the newspaper he'd lifted earlier from the café. Time would tell if she was connected.

He finished his meal, pushed the plate to one side and looked round, catching the woman's eye.

'Good?' she asked, looking slightly amused.

'Not bad. Filled a gap.'

He seemed to have his chance. She'd finished texting. They had spoken.

'Staying long?' he asked.

She shook her head. 'Just a couple of days. How about you?'

'Oh, I live here.'

'It seems a nice place.'

'It is, yes. A bit quiet for you, though, I would have thought.'

'For me? Oh, I can do quiet,' she said briskly. 'It suits me nicely.'

She said nothing else. It wasn't long before she got up to go.

He couldn't make his mind up about her. Was he just being paranoid again?

And he wondered if he'd done the right thing, keeping quiet all day. Why hadn't he reported what had happened? Who to, though? The local police? Will Taylor? He smiled grimly at the thought. Will would have had a heart attack.

If he'd kept in touch with the Service, he could have contacted someone there, but he hadn't. He hadn't wanted to. Anyway, the Service didn't encourage former operatives to stay in touch. It hadn't the interest or the resources to become a care provider for ex-employees.

The woman paused by his table on her way out. 'Jake Ord, isn't it?' she said quietly. Without waiting for a response, she added, 'As a very special favour to me, Jake, can I ask you to keep out of the way? Please!'

His heart began thumping, but he managed not to look astonished, or to follow her with his eyes when she moved on.

So he'd been right, he thought with grim satisfaction. She was connected.

She chuckled to herself as she made her way up to her room. It had taken her a while to get a half-decent photo, but she'd persevered and eventually got a couple of shots of him. They were poor, blurred images, but almost full-face and about as good as she would expect on her old camera phone. She'd forwarded them, and hadn't had long to wait.

Jake Ord. Retired. Overseas operations specialist. No longer active.

Not positively inactive, though, she thought with a frown. He'd picked her out easily enough. Spotted her straight away. That was bloody disappointing.

Back in her room, she put her mobile on the charger and sat thoughtfully for a couple of minutes. At least her instincts had been good. That was something. She hadn't kept bumping into him, or he into her, by accident.

He had picked her out though, she thought again. That wasn't good. She grimaced and wondered what she'd done wrong. Maybe she didn't make a convincing tourist.

She also wondered whether to seek advice, but decided against it. As yet, she'd hardly started. Who knew what Jake Ord was doing here?

CHAPTER SIX

He stood outside, on the steps of The King's Arms, and gazed at the Land Rover. He was still in two minds, if not more. He was ready to go. He could get in the Land Rover right now and move out. There was nothing keeping him here. Nothing at all. He been here for three years, but that was all. It wasn't as if he belonged here. It wasn't even as if Ellie had ever been here. He'd just stuck a pin in the map, with his eyes closed, and hit it. Cragley.

He was quite capable of doing that again. Some other pin. Some other map. He could disappear again. Find some other retreat. He could even just go to Uncle Bob's old place in Cleveland. Get some sea air. Do some fishing. The place was his now. It was time he went; he hadn't been since the old chap died.

He could. He could move on. There wasn't such a lot keeping him here. What had he done in these last three years? Lived, mostly. Just lived. He'd tried his hand at a bit of painting. There were his books, as well. His book collection. How many books? Fifty, maybe? A hundred? It wasn't a lot to show anybody, not for three years invested in a place.

There was Apache, as well, of course, he thought with a rueful smile and a shake of the head. Some of the time he had Apache for company. When Apache wasn't out hunting or seeking females.

No. Fuck it! He wasn't going to run. This was his home now. Anyway, he wanted to know what was going on. If he left now, he might never know.

And plenty was going on. It hadn't started just today either. Or last night, for that matter. And most definitely it hadn't started with the young blonde woman in The King's Arms, the one who knew his name even though he didn't know hers.

He'd first sensed it three weeks' ago, on holiday. That was when his unease had become impossible to ignore, and when he'd first had evidence it was justified.

Majorca. A perfectly nice place in the north of the island, near the mountains. Even a perfectly nice woman he'd met in a bar there. Then it had started, and hadn't stopped. The feeling that something wasn't quite right. The sense that he was being watched. Little things that didn't add up.

Maids moved things when they cleaned and tidied rooms. They had to. It was to be expected, but usually they didn't go through pockets and look inside suitcases. Or study passports and put them back the wrong way round. Not normally, they didn't. And normally he didn't feel eyes on him all the time.

After a day or two, he'd got rid of the woman and didn't invite her to his room any more. A small rudeness had been enough. She'd taken the hint. It was a pity, but he hadn't wanted her in the way, in harm's way. Afterwards, he'd just sat for a day, waiting. Then he'd moved out. Fast and unexpectedly.

A day later he'd seen the results of the fire as he drove by in his rented car. The roof was gone. Several rooms burned out. He guessed an incendiary device had started it. Possibly there had been a small explosive device, as well, but he hadn't stopped to enquire.

He'd left altogether then, left the island and come home. And been especially vigilant. More so than usual. Now someone had tried to nail him here with a high-powered rifle. And not far away someone else had died in a fire. And the mysterious blonde woman knew his name.

No connection, of course. Pure coincidence, but he didn't think so. Something was going on, and he seemed to be in the middle of it. So he wasn't going to run. He was going to see it through. He'd decided.

'Nice night.'

He looked over his shoulder at Tom Fairbrother and nodded, 'And warm enough.'

'Away home now, Jake?'

He hesitated. 'Tom, are you full at the moment?'

'Full? Why no! We're never full. Plenty of room, if you want to stay.'

It was intended as a joke, but Jake didn't laugh. 'I wouldn't mind taking you up on that, Tom. I'm having some work done at the cottage, and it's got to the point where it might be sensible to move out for a few days.'

'Any time,' Tom said, turning to go back inside.

Jake nodded. He might be back sooner than Tom realized. Not least because he wanted to know how the hell the blonde woman knew his name.

Heading back to the Land Rover, he spotted the familiar bulky shape of Cedric meandering across the green with Rupert, his ancient Labrador. He grimaced. He really didn't want to talk to Cedric just now. Instinct told him to keep well away from friends. He wanted them to stay alive.

'Nice evening, Jake.'

'Not bad, Ced.'

The other man headed across the road to join him. 'On your way home?'

'On my way.'

Cedric peered at him curiously. 'Special occasion, is it?'

'Not really. Things to do. That's all.'

'But you're still here?'

'Still here!' Jake waved a hand and carried on walking.

He felt the other man's eyes on his retreating back but he kept going without looking round. The last thing he wanted was to involve Cedric and Caitlin in whatever trouble was pursuing him.

He slowed the Land Rover on the way back to the cottage, turned off the track along the little valley and stopped in the lee of a hawthorn thicket. He sat for a few moments, considering. Then he got out, locked up and took to the sheep trails on the hillside. In the gathering gloom he made his way uphill, until he was just below the skyline, and then he moved northwards, parallel to the track.

It was slow going. The light was good enough for sky gazing, but poor for the careful traversing of rough ground, especially if you didn't want to make any noise.

Probably the caution was unnecessary. They'd had their chance and messed up, and would have moved on by now. Gone away, far away. Given up.

He hoped, but he didn't believe it. He wasn't a great fan of wishful thinking. Whoever it was would try again. If they'd picked him up in Majorca and followed him here, they wouldn't give up now. Not yet.

He came to a stop. The cottage was in sight. At least, it would have been if it hadn't been so dark down in the valley, but he could see where it should be. It formed a patch of particularly heavy darkness in the distance, and he recognised the shape of the skyline above it.

The scene looked peaceful enough. There was no light, no noise, no sign of anything at all out of the ordinary. Nothing. He was almost disappointed.

He continued to stare down into the darkness, trying to visualize and follow in his mind's eye the course of the track that led along the valley to the cottage, and then up to the old quarry. He no longer expected to find anyone here but it seemed sensible to tread carefully anyway, just in case.

As he began to move again, he heard a sound suggesting he might have reached a premature conclusion, something suggesting he might not be alone. He stopped and turned his head slightly, to use his peripheral vision. Nothing. He could see nothing at all. It was like looking into a black bag.

The sound had come from somewhere lower on the hillside, somewhere between him and the track. It wasn't much, a very faint sound, but he hadn't imagined it. He knew that. It could have been a badger. Or someone clearing their throat.

Hard as he stared, he could see nothing. The noise had come from somewhere down there, faint but carried unmistakably on the still evening air. He hesitated a moment longer and then began a cautious, crouching descent, his pulse racing now.

Fronds of bracken tickled his face. Heather tugged at his ankles and tried to hold him back. Birch twigs brushed against his chest. It was tough going. He edged his way down the steep slope, feeling ahead gingerly with each foot before he set it down, ready to drop flat at any moment.

It became darker than ever. Not up above, where he could see the skyline and starlight, but down-slope where he could see next to nothing. The pool of darkness where the sound had come from was impenetrable – no light, no movement, and no further sound now. Nothing at all.

He knew he hadn't imagined it, though. He stuck to that thought. Someone was there, somewhere nearby.

He sank to the ground when he was thirty feet or so above where he believed the track to be. He sat still and waited.

The minutes ticked by. Once or twice he strained to hear more when some faint sound carried to his ears. The stirring of an almost imperceptible breeze. The slow, gentle rustling of leaves. The creak of bracken bending and shrivelling as the night air cooled. He made a conscious effort to relax, to ease into the ground, to feel and listen, to become part of the night. It was a while since he'd last done this, but there had been a time when he was good at it.

A stronger breeze arose after a little while and began to stir the leaves in a nearby clump of small birch trees more vigorously. He used the disturbance as cover to stretch and ease himself. But he didn't leave his position. He wouldn't move from it without more information.

Then he got it. A dim glow of light appeared below and some twenty feet to his left. He heard what sounded like a mobile phone being activated. He gave a grim smile of satisfaction. He hadn't been wasting his time.

He edged closer. He could hear fragments of whispered conversation. Someone demanding to know what was going on.

Of course! The sniper had a spotter, presumably based in the village. Jake wondered who it was. The blonde woman, perhaps? Possibly, but he didn't think so now, not since she'd spoken to him. It would have to be someone unseen, someone he hadn't noticed.

He guessed they were in a quandary. They didn't know where he was and were worried about it. He'd dropped off their radar.

He moved quickly while the whispers continued, using the distraction to get close and preparing to attack. He waited until the conversation had ended and the phone was switched off, then he sprang forward the last few feet.

The man heard him coming, but it was too late for him to do much about it. Jake slammed into him, looped an arm around his throat from behind and pulled him back off balance.

The man lashed backwards with his heel but Jake had anticipated the move and avoided it. He could feel he was bigger and stronger than his opponent, and he stretched until the man was scarcely touching the ground. Arms flailed at him. 'Keep still, or I'll break your bloody neck!' he growled.

The flailing stopped.

Then a powerful light hit him full in the face. He winced and ducked his head, dazzled. He was shocked. He'd assumed there was only one of them. Wrong assumption!

It all happened so fast then, too fast to make sense of. There was no time to think; Jake instinctively hurtled forward towards the light, using the struggling figure he held in front of him as a shield.

They hit another body and a tangle of limbs. The light left Jake's face and fell to the ground. He heard the dull whump-whump of a handgun fitted with a silencer – two shots. The man he held arched and kicked in a violent spasm when the bullets hit. Jake hurled him forward and dived sideways. Then he was rolling fast downhill.

He dropped over a low lip of rock and crashed heavily to the ground below, jarring his spine agonisingly and cracking his head. Ignoring the pain, he scuttled sideways into high bracken and kept moving. When his energy flagged, he dropped and lay flat. He bit into the sleeve of his jacket, to quieten his gasping breath.

There was a lot of flailing around on the hillside above his position. No voices, but the sounds of a search and light. Someone was looking for him. Jake kept his head down and did the next best thing to praying.

Presently the light and the sounds moved away. He stayed still until he was sure no-one was close. Then he began to crawl back uphill, hoping whoever had been waiting for him would expect him to be making for the track.

Only one of them was left now, he thought grimly. The man he'd held wasn't one to worry about any more. He'd felt his neck go, even if the bullets hadn't done the job first.

So it had really started now, he told himself grimly, and he was a player, not just a victim.

CHAPTER SEVEN

Jake worked his way well clear of the ambush site and then headed fast along the track, back to where he'd left the Land Rover. He was thinking hard as he went. So it wasn't one man, a lone sniper. There had been two, and the two had been in conversation with a third. No reason why the ones he knew about were the only ones either. So the situation looked different – worse.

He needed help. He knew that now. The question was which way to turn.

There still didn't seem much point in involving the police. The locals didn't have the capability themselves, and by the time they'd called in the Met's Special Branch, or whoever it was now – if they did – it could well be too late.

There was always his old employer, but he'd lost touch. He'd walked out on them. He'd done his bit. More in fact. More than could reasonably be expected. And he'd lost Ellie. Or they had. It had been time to move on.

He doubted if his old contacts would still be there anyway. Retirement, restructuring, operational mortality, and unexplained disappearances would all have taken their toll. After three years he wouldn't be remembered at all.

Where else could he turn for help?

The answer to his problem came to him as he reached the Land Rover. A name and a face: Dixie! He smiled at last and started the engine. As he drove back into Cragley, heading for a room at the King's Arms, he thought about her and nodded with satisfaction. Then he frowned as he wondered how difficult she would be to find.

*

He booked into The King's Arms, got settled in his room and took out his mobile. It took him the best part of an hour but he did find her.

'Jake!'

'You're hard to track down, Dixie.'

'I like it that way.'

'But I've found you at last.'

'I'm so glad. How are you, Jake?'

He enjoyed hearing her voice. He enjoyed being able to talk to her. This was one person, he knew for sure, who was on his side. Besides, she was good at what she did, very good.

'I'm still in one piece, Dixie. Just.'

'Oh? Trouble?'

'Afraid so.'

'Need help?'

'Just a bit.'

'I'll come. Where are you?'

He told her. She'd had no idea. Nor would anyone else from the old days have had.

'You'll have to give me a little time, Jake. Probably twelve hours. Maybe less.'

That meant she was back on the other side of the Atlantic. Out west, probably. He told her where he'd meet her. It wouldn't be here.

Afterwards, he smiled happily. Dixie had that effect on him. She always did have. There had been a time when he might have hooked up with her instead of Ellie, her friend, but it had been Ellie he couldn't stay away from, Ellie with her fun-loving, extrovert style. Her death had put an end to a lot of things, including his time in the Service. After she'd gone, he'd just wanted out.

Dixie hadn't mentioned Ellie. She wouldn't. It was her way. She'd moved on, and expected other people to do the same. Never look back. It was a brave maxim. One he aspired to keep himself.

Jake went down to the bar. Tom was wearily polishing glasses. He looked up. 'Everything all right?'

'Fine.' Jake nodded. 'Nice and quiet up there.'

'Should be. There's just one other guest at the moment.'

'That woman who was having a meal earlier?'

Tom shook his head. 'Dave, he's called. He's here every other week.'

Jake nodded. That was that, then. She wasn't here. The mystery blonde woman. He ordered a shot of Famous Grouse. He might as well. He felt in need of something bracing.

He noticed Will Taylor, the sergeant, over in a corner, next to the dying fire. He was on his own and looked as if he didn't want company. He moved over to join him anyway.

'Tough day?'

Will looked up and nodded. 'So-so.'

'Fellside Farm. It sounded like a bad accident?'

'Aye. If that's what it was.'

'Is there any doubt?'

'I'm just an old-fashioned copper,' Will said wearily. 'I'm no detective. But I'll be surprised if the clever boys coming tomorrow conclude it was an accident.'

'Oh?'

'Big, expensive motors don't just burst into flames when they're being driven at five miles an hour. And even if they do, the driver usually has time to get out.'

Jake agreed. 'So what. . . ?'

'I haven't a clue, mate. I've never seen anything like it. I don't want to again, either. It wasn't nice.'

He finished his pint and shuffled, getting ready to stand up.

'Who was he?'

Will shrugged. 'Nobody seems to know much about him. Nice enough fellow, by all accounts, but quiet. Kept himself to himself, if you know what I mean. A bit like you, Jake.'

Jake smiled uneasily.

'Anyway,' Will added, 'I've got a man out there now, and another to relieve him in a while. Then I'll go back myself. We'll keep the site under guard till the clever boys get here tomorrow.'

'From Ponteland?'

'Ponteland be buggered! The Northumbria Police can't handle this, apparently. Oh, no!' He shook his head and snorted with derision. 'They're coming from London. What used to be Special Branch. How do you like that?'

Definitely not a coincidence, then, Jake thought as he watched Will plod across the room and shoulder his way through the door and out into the night. Special Branch? From London? Something was definitely going on.

CHAPTER EIGHT

'Grady didn't make it.'

'Tell me.'

The tall, thin man, whose name was Scobie, told him. The boss man listened without interrupting.

'So you cocked it up – again!'

'Well. . . .'

'You cocked it up.'

Scobie didn't even try to deny it a second time. He waited. It was out of his hands. There was nothing he could do now anyway.

'This is getting more complicated than I'd hoped,' the boss man said with a sigh.

His tone was surprisingly mild. Scobie hoped he was simply preoccupied with the technical problems.

'Grey and Williams will come in to sort it out,' the other man resumed. 'They'll move the body. Then they'll stay. From now on I want you to concentrate on your primary task. Forget about everything else. Forget Ord. They can handle him. You stay put – and stay focussed.'

Scobie was relieved. The heavy, strong-arm stuff wasn't his bag anyway. Let the others handle it. He'd get back to base and prepare. He needed to. His timing wasn't right. It still rankled that he'd missed when the target had been in his sights.

The trouble was he'd shot either too soon or too late. He wouldn't have missed if the target had been outside. He should have waited, or taken the earlier opportunity. Next time he'd get it right. He'd better, or he'd be out of work. Or worse.

CHAPTER NINE

Friday morning: the village was busy. It was inundated in fact, with farmers and their wives who'd come from the outlying areas. The scene was like a carnival; Jake watched it all without much interest.

He was stuck and didn't know what to do next. He was out of ideas. Unless the sniper took another pop at him, or the woman who knew his name re-appeared, there wasn't much he could do. There was nothing to research; nowhere to look; no-one to pursue. Stuck. Worried, and stuck.

He called in at The Gallery, where Caitlin was cleaning brushes and Cedric was studying *The Times* crossword. Cedric had a cigarette dangling from one corner of his mouth, implying concentration as well as defiance of the grown-up consensus on smoking.

'Here again, Jake?' Caitlin said with surprise and a bright smile. She broke off to dry her hands on an old cloth. 'Two days running? Aren't we the lucky ones?'

'Here again,' Jake admitted. 'How's Apache?'

'Still in the cellar, enjoying the hunt.'

'He'll get rid of the mice for you. I have every confidence in him, but you'd better watch he doesn't see Rupert off, as well.'

'Oh, Rupert doesn't mind him. He's a very laid-back dog, is Rupert, even for a Lab. He can take care of himself.'

Jake turned to Cedric, who was quietly thinking about something. Possibly something starting with a Q and having sixteen letters, ending with a Z.

'All right, Cedric?'

'All right, Jake. Thank you.' Cedric re-settled his spectacles and added,

'You're out and about early?'

'Thought I might pick up a cup of coffee if I timed it right.'

Cedric didn't respond. Jake wondered what he had on his mind.

Caitlin said, 'I was just going to put some coffee on.'

'Anything much happening?' Jake asked airily after she had departed for the kitchen.

'Not a thing,' Cedric said. 'Village quiet as ever, but you should know that.'

'Me?'

'I assume you stayed the night at the pub?'

Jake nodded and yawned. 'I did, yes.'

'Not like you.'

'Couldn't resist the lure of the bright lights.'

Jake felt uneasy, as if he were under friendly interrogation. It was awkward. Cedric seemed suspicious but there was nothing he could tell him without involving him, which was the last thing he wanted to do. It would be far too dangerous. He shouldn't really even be here.

'I just fancied a change, Ced. That's all.'

'Not like you,' Cedric repeated.

Jake smiled politely.

'Well, I'm not surprised,' Caitlin said, bustling in with a tray. 'I don't know how you stick it out there all the time.'

'At the cottage? Oh, it has its compensations.'

'Never fancy moving into civilisation?'

Jake smiled. 'Here, you mean?'

'You could do worse.'

'I'm sure I could. In fact, I know I could.'

Cedric was still watching him closely. Jake didn't like that. It put him in an invidious position. He didn't want to lie to his friends. On the other hand, he didn't want to worry them either. Or put them in danger.

He drank the coffee, declined the offer from Caitlin of lunch and left without seeing Apache. He'd best stay away until this thing was finished, he decided.

He wandered along the street until he reached the chemist's shop. Then he paused and studied the orthopaedic sandals in the window. They were on sale. Half-price. End of season. He wondered how long it would be before he needed special footwear like that, and found himself hoping he lived that long.

Reflected in a mirror on a shelf behind the window he saw Cedric paddling along towards him, Rupert in tow. He waited until they were close before turning with a ready smile.

Cedric didn't smile back. He stopped, stood still and spoke quietly but firmly. 'Keep your trouble away from us, Jake. Whatever it is, don't you bring it onto our doorstep!'

'Cedric! Trouble?' Jake began to protest with alarm.

'I mean it. We'll look after your cat for you, but keep away from us.'

'What makes you think I've got trouble?'

Cedric twitched his head impatiently and turned away. Over his shoulder, he added, 'You're not welcome any more, Jake.'

Jake watched him waddle away, and felt the emptiness growing inside him. He wondered how he had ever allowed himself to believe you could count on friends.

CHAPTER TEN

She was small and neat. Compact. Strong. Quick-moving and well coordinated. Athletic. And pretty? Oh, yes! She was that, all right. That, as well.

Not full-on beautiful, perhaps, but a good-looking woman who shone with energy and fitness. Yet . . . Yet, for all that, she was unremarkable to look at if you didn't study her, and recognize her qualities – which was exactly how they had always wanted it to be in their game.

But he didn't need to study her. He knew her. And he knew she was remarkable.

He watched her walking along the platform towards him. She was one of only half a dozen passengers to alight from the London train at Alnmouth Station. She had a backpack slung on her right shoulder and she carried a hold-all in her left hand. He could see the smile on her face from thirty yards away. He smiled back.

Her pace didn't quicken but, unlike her fellow passengers, she looked fresh and full of running. And unlike them she'd had a long flight even before boarding the train.

Her hair was different from the last time he'd seen her. She was no longer blonde. She was a natural dark brown again now, but her hair was still cut short and manageable. There would be a name for the style, he supposed, but to him it was just sensible and practical. Easy to dry. Not much for the wind to wrap across her face or whip into her eyes. Not much to get hold of at close quarters either – practical.

She wore outdoor trousers with lots of zips, light-weight walking boots, and a brown sweater under a dark-green field jacket. She was tanned by sun and wind. She looked good.

'Dixie!' he murmured when she was close enough to hear.

The smile escalated and lit up her face like a welcoming beacon. She dropped the hold-all and the rucksack, and came in close to give him a hug. He squeezed back gently, carefully, letting her make the pace. She'd never been big on bodily contact.

'So good to see you, Jake.'

'And you, Dixie. You're a sight for sore eyes.'

She laughed. 'They must be real sore, those eyes of yours.'

'Oh, they are! Believe me. How was your trip? Exhausting?'

'Not really. Not at all, in fact.' She broke away from him and pulled back. She didn't like fuss. 'You got a car?'

He nodded. He'd brought the elderly, cherished BMW he kept garaged in the village, so it didn't have to run the gauntlet of the track to the cottage.

'Let's go,' she suggested.

'Sure. Hungry?'

'I guess I am, yeah. I could eat. Drink, too.'

'OK.'

He stooped and grabbed her hold-all. 'We'll have a meal at the hotel I've booked you into in Alnmouth.'

'Not your place?'

He shook his head. 'I'll explain later.'

He steered her towards the exit. Already they were the only people still on the platform. The train had gone and he could hear cars starting up in the adjacent car park. Alnmouth was tiny, and the station just outside it no more than a halt.

They said little on the short journey into the village. No point starting a conversation that was going to be interrupted soon.

The White Horse was an old coaching inn set in the main street in Alnmouth, a village located in the lonely corner where the River Aln met the sea. Historic, picturesque Alnmouth was a quiet place of singular beauty. When you could see it.

'Nice!' Dixie said, standing on the pavement outside the entrance to the hotel, glancing at the sign hanging overhead and then looking along the street. Peering through the fog bank.

'Old,' Jake said. 'Falling to bits.'

'Right.'

She spun round again. 'No casino?'

'Not one.'

She nodded, as if vaguely disappointed.

'Sorry about the visibility,' he ventured. 'But it is, "the season of mist". . . .'

' "And mellow fruitfulness"?' she added with a grin.

'Exactly. Off the sea, at this time of year—'

'Come on!' she laughed. 'It's beautiful. I love it.'

He shepherded her inside, and wondered where she'd been recently. Not a hint of perfume. So she'd been working. Somewhere. He didn't ask.

After she'd registered, he said, 'Right. You've got thirty minutes to brush your teeth and comb your hair. I'll be in the Residents' Lounge, working up an appetite.'

'Fifteen will do. My teeth aren't that dirty, and I just shake my hair.'

He smiled. 'Take as long as you need, Dixie. I'll be here.'

'So what's going on, Jake?'

She had finished her grilled salmon and salad and he'd finished his sirloin steak and peas, leaving most of the chips. They had both skipped dessert. The coffee was plentiful and good. They were ready to talk. He told her, everything.

'Has anything like this ever happened before?' she asked when he'd finished.

He shook his head. 'But I'm not too surprised. I've always half-expected it.'

'So you never really got free of the Service?'

He shook his head. 'I wonder if you ever really can, people like us.'

'Perhaps not.' She shook her head. 'Be sure your sin will find you out.'

'No sins, Dixie. We were the good guys. You, at least, still are, aren't you?'

She shrugged. 'I hope so, Jake. I really do hope so.'

'You are,' he told her firmly. 'And so was I. And so was Ellie. Maybe not everyone is, but we were then. And you are now.'

She nodded. 'You're right. OK. But someone's gunning for you. Any idea who?'

'Until I get more information, I haven't a clue.'

She looked thoughtful and tapped her fingers on her chin. He remembered that mannerism. She was thinking.

'It's a strange coincidence,' she suggested, 'that someone else living in an isolated cottage, and not far away, has just been killed, isn't it? Accident or not.'

'Very strange.'

'And on the same night that someone took a shot at you,' she added, peering thoughtfully at him.

He nodded.

'Maybe it's not a coincidence at all. Have you considered that possibility, Jake? Any connection with you, this guy?'

'None that I'm aware of. I didn't know him at all. I didn't even know he existed. All I do know is that this "accident", or whatever it was, actually happened. He's dead.'

He showed her Cragley on the 1:50,000 map and then where his cottage was. He also pointed out the spot where some poor unfortunate had died in his 4-by-4. The distance between the two locations was a good five miles. Nearer ten, if you took account of road distance.

Dixie said: 'Let's assume, for the moment, your friendly local cop is right, and it wasn't an accident. Could someone have thought the other guy was you?'

'Mistaken identity?' Jake shrugged. 'Who knows?'

He'd wondered about that himself.

'Depends on the timing, doesn't it?' he added. 'If his "accident" happened first, then possibly. They may have realized their mistake and come after me, but if they went for me first, then no. They'd have found who they were after.'

'Unless it was him they wanted all along?' Dixie suggested. 'The attempted hit on you could have been the mistake. When they realized it, they went over there and completed the job.'

'But then they wouldn't have had a second go at me, would they? The ambush?'

'Just cleaning up? Loose ends?'

'Maybe.'

He nodded. It could have been like that, but until they got more information they were just fumbling and speculating.

'Or they wanted the both of you,' Dixie persisted. 'They got him, but not you.'

'So I'm unfinished business?'

Dixie nodded.

He sighed and shook his head. 'Maybe it was just an accident.'

'Maybe it was.'

They were quiet for a few moments then, worn out by the circularity of their hypothetical discussion.

Dixie started up again. 'So maybe it really was a coincidence? The attack on you and the accident to him.'

'Yeah, but they're serious about me,' Jake pointed out. 'They've been on my trail for a while. I told you about Majorca.'

They stared at the map some more. Then Dixie said, 'Tell me about the woman again, the one that warned you off.'

He told her again.

'So she knew your name. Could she have overheard someone saying it?'

He cast his mind back and shook his head. 'I don't think so. My first name maybe, but not my second. At least, no-one used it when I was around.'

'So she took the trouble to find out. She asked.' Dixie looked up at him, a twinkle in her eye. 'Do you find that happens a lot with strange, unknown women?'

'Not as often as I would like,' he told her with a grin, and in all modesty.

'Poor Jake!'

For a moment he wondered if she was thinking of Ellie. Then she laughed. So did he. They didn't speak of Ellie, which for him was hard. He would have liked to talk about her. He was no longer in touch with anyone else who had known her.

'So Mystery Woman took the trouble to find out who you were, or she knew already,' Dixie mused.

'And she warned me off, in the nicest possible way.'

'So something is going on, and she's involved.'

He agreed but he didn't know what the connection was. He didn't know where the woman had gone either, which was a pity. He wanted to question her.

'The two guys who ambushed you,' Dixie said, changing tack again. 'Maybe they had each taken a target, and after one had been successful he came to help out his partner.'

Jake didn't bother commenting. It was just wild speculation, of which they didn't really need any more.

'So what do you want me to do?' Dixie asked when she grew tired of speculating.

'Deep cover. Hunt around. See what you can pick up. Someone's out there. Something's going on. We need to know who they are and what it is.'

'Have you considered just moving out, Jake? Moving out and covering your trail?'

'Briefly.'

They both knew he could do that. Go on the run. Disappear again. The trouble was he'd spent three years getting his life back, and he'd come to like it now he had. It wasn't a perfect life, maybe, but it was good enough. And a hell of a lot better than it had been. The other stuff, the other life, was behind him now. Or so he'd hoped.

'This is home now, Dixie. My home. I like it here.'

She nodded. 'I guessed. You're . . . what? Happy?'

'I suppose I am. Yes. In my own way.'

'What do you do in that cottage, Jake? When you're not dodging bullets?'

'Not much,' he admitted, 'but I'm getting there. I've taken up painting, for example.'

'Nice.'

He didn't tell her what a struggle it had been after Ellie had got herself

NEVER LOOK BACK · 49

killed. After that his world had crumbled. Dixie would know anyway. She could guess.

'What's it like,' she asked gently, 'having somewhere you call home?'

'Good. I'm going back there,' he added, before she could again suggest moving on.

'I must come and see this cottage of yours.'

'Later,' he said briskly. 'When it's safe.'

She nodded. 'Jake, is there another reason you don't want to leave, apart from the home thing?'

He started to tell her that he wanted to know what was going on. He didn't want to just pull up his fledgling roots and disappear to start all over again. He stopped, realizing she meant something else.

'No,' he said gently. 'There's no-one else in my life. How about you?'

She shook her head. 'We're two of a kind, Jake, you and me,' she said sadly.

'That's not all bad.'

'No, of course it isn't,' she said, giving him a smile that hid whatever else she was feeling.

'We used to be good at getting things done,' he pointed out.

'I am still,' she countered. 'How about you?'

'We'll see,' he said with a laugh, rising to the challenge.

She grinned. 'Oh, boy! I can hardly wait.'

CHAPTER ELEVEN

Jake returned to Cragley, leaving Dixie in Alnmouth. He had no qualms about that. Dixie preferred to be left alone to get on with things. It was what she was good at.

He smiled with satisfaction and pleasure. He was lucky she'd been able to take time out. For a moment he wondered what he'd pulled her away from. There was no telling. She wouldn't have said, and he couldn't guess. He wouldn't ask either. Although he was no longer part of that world he still respected its rules.

His mind moved on. He was puzzled and worried by Cedric's little outburst that morning. What on earth had that been about? It seemed so out of character. And how had Cedric guessed he was in trouble? Had it been that obvious? Even if it had, he would have expected Cedric to offer help, not to warn him to stay away.

How much did he really know about Cedric and Caitlin? Not a lot. He knew they had been here some years and he knew about The Gallery. He knew they had hitherto always been unfailingly pleasant and friendly, but that was about it. That was all he did know.

He'd never asked about anything else either, partly because he didn't want them asking about his life. Chickens coming home to roost, he thought with a wry smile. You need to know your friends before you lean on them.

Cragley was quiet. The streets were empty. The pubs darkened. The antique street lamps cast a sad, misty light over the parked cars and the village green. Hard to believe anything unpleasant could happen in this neighbourhood. It seemed incredible that this was a place where people got shot at, and sometimes burned to death in their cars.

The King's Arms was still open for business, but only just. Tom was in the bar, talking to the one remaining customer.

'Join us?' Tom called. 'Nightcap?'

Jake hesitated. He didn't want a drink. Tom took down a fresh glass and poured a Bell's that he placed on the counter, alongside the two others that were there. It would have been churlish to decline.

Jake joined the two of them at the bar.

'You know Colin, don't you?' Tom said.

He didn't. He nodded and shook Colin's hand. Colin looked relieved to get it back. He looked, in fact, as if he'd had a trying day. Perhaps a trying life.

'Colin's had a tough day,' Tom said, as if seeing what was on Jake's mind.

'I've known better,' Colin agreed.

Jake looked from one to the other of them.

'He's an ambulance man,' Tom explained.

'Paramedic,' Colin corrected him.

'Paramedic.' Tom nodded. 'That's it.' He sipped his whisky and added, 'That fellow out at Fellside Farm cottage.'

Jake's interest heightened. 'You've been out there?' he asked, turning to Colin.

'All day, nearly.'

'To reclaim the body,' Tom added.

'What was left of it,' Colin reminded him.

'Aye. What was left of it.' Tom patted him on the shoulder.

Colin, understandably, seemed to have been unnerved by the experience. 'It wasn't nice,' he said, eyeing the Bell's bottle. 'Not nice at all.'

Tom took the hint and reached for the bottle. 'Interesting, though,' he said to Jake. 'The man didn't die in the crash or the fire, apparently. So the police reckon, anyway.'

'That right?'

Colin nodded. 'They reckon he was shot first – shot dead.'

'In his vehicle?'

'Aye,' Colin said with a doleful look.

So he really hadn't been the only target, Jake thought. He almost felt relieved.

The next morning Jake decided to cut through all the confusion and speculation. He would start at the one obvious place to start. He would check out the other target, the one the shooters had managed to put down.

The track to the farm was closed. A police car stood nearby, making sure the sign was respected. Jake turned back and cut across fields.

Fellside Farm was sheltered from the prevailing westerly winds by a horse-shoe of Scots Pine. The farmhouse and adjacent farm buildings were visible through the trees. So was a short terrace of three or four small stone cottages, built in a bygone age when farms had many men to work them.

He stood and studied the layout for a few minutes, getting the feel of it. He felt better than recently – alert and vigorous. No longer worried and confused, he was doing something, something positive at last.

There were vehicles in sight near the farmhouse: a battered and muddy pick-up, a smart tractor with a covered cab for the driver and a white van – no Land Rover, though, and no people. There were no dogs roaming around either, which was a blessing.

There were no vehicles outside the cottages. Particularly, there were no vehicles with police markings. That was good. He wasn't looking for extra trouble.

Nothing new struck him about the farm buildings. Time to go. He set off for the farmhouse, to see if he could get some questions answered directly.

A young, overweight woman came to the door. She was carrying a baby and had a child not much older clinging to her skirt. She was smiling, which seemed a happy omen. Jake smiled back.

'Sorry to bother you,' he began. 'You look busy. I should have come at another time.'

'You wouldn't have caught me not being busy,' she assured him with a laugh. 'If it's our Jacky you want, he's away to Alnwick this morning. He's gone to see his mam.'

That helped.

'Oh, I am disappointed!' Jake said, trying to look as if he truly was.

'He'll be back this afternoon, if that's any good?'

Jake shook his head, grimaced and then looked at the woman hopefully. 'I just wanted some information about the cottage.'

She looked puzzled. 'How do you mean?'

'The cottage for let – or is it for sale? I'm not sure which.'

'Here? There's nothing available here.' She paused and added, 'There might be one coming up for let in the future, though, I suppose. Our tenant was killed in an accident just the other day.'

'Not. . . .' Jake nodded down the track. 'Back there?'

She grimaced. 'I'm afraid so. His vehicle caught fire. He couldn't get out, poor man, and by the time Jacky reached the blaze it was too late. He was very upset about it. He is still. That's why. . . .'

She broke off, considered and then said, 'I'm surprised the police let you past. They said they would be stopping everyone but us while they did their investigation.'

'I had to leave my car,' Jake told her.

'You walked? All that way?'

'It's not far. And I like walking. Well, thanks for your time. I'd better be getting back. If you don't mind, I'll just walk round the cottages while I'm here, in case one does come up sometime in the future.'

'Feel free. No problem. I'd show you inside myself but I've got my hands full at the moment. I probably shouldn't anyway with Mr Sanderson. . . .' she added uncertainly.

'Don't worry about it,' Jake said with a shrug. He turned to study the row of cottages. 'Four cottages? Which one was your tenant's?'

'There're only two cottages now. They were knocked together. Mr Sanderson had the one at the far end, on a long let. The one at this end is a holiday cottage we let out by the week. It's empty now. You could look round that one yourself, if you like? They're both the same.'

'Could I? Thank you. I'd appreciate it.'

She went away and returned with a bunch of keys. 'Number Two,' she said, fingering one of the keys.

He guessed the one very like it was for Number One. His luck was in.

*

He didn't spend much time in Number Two cottage. He opened up, took a quick look around in case Jacky's wife was watching and then used the companion key to get into Number One. Surprisingly, the place wasn't festooned with crime-scene tape. Sergeant Will Taylor's clever boys from London couldn't have arrived yet.

In itself, that raised a question. Why was anyone at all coming from London? What was so special about this 'accident', or even murder, that it required the attention of the Met? Assuming it actually was murder, it had to be something out of the ordinary. The Met wouldn't be coming all this way otherwise.

The two cottages were virtually identical. They each comprised a pair of cottages that had been knocked into one now there was no need for farm labourers and their teeming families. The two resultant cottages were still pretty small and basic, but cosy enough. There were two bedrooms apiece, a decent-sized living-room, a kitchen with dining area, and a bathroom. They were both equipped for modern living, with a fridge-freezer, washing machine, dryer and television. Plus as much cheerful, modern furniture as a short-term tenant who didn't mind IKEA style was likely to want.

Number One had a few extra items, presumably installed by the long-term tenant, but not many. There was a small Persian rug that looked genuine in the living room, on top of the wall-to-wall beige carpet. A portable radio stood on the kitchen work-top. There was also a framed print on the living room wall that didn't look landlord-supplied. It was a landscape, but not one to be found around these parts – a hot desert scene.

He ran his eye over things quickly, touching as little as possible. Forensics might be here soon. He didn't want to spoil things for them. Or add his prints to whatever were already here.

Several copies of the *Telegraph* were piled neatly on the coffee table in the living-room. A small collection of books occupied a shelf fixed to one wall. Nothing out of the ordinary there. There were a couple of paper-backs, mainstream popular titles out of recent top-twenty lists; an RSPB pocket book on bird identification; a 'Castles of Northumberland' and an A-Z for Newcastle. Sanderson had not been much of a reader.

In the kitchen Jake could see nothing that had not come supplied with the cottage, except a sparse assortment of fresh food in the fridge-freezer and a large collection of tinned stuff in one cupboard. Clearly the former occupant hadn't been a gourmet either. Or a drinker. There was no sign of alcohol of any description.

Only one bedroom seemed to have been in use. The double bed there was neatly made. The room was tidy. Everything had been put away, nothing at all left out. It made Jake wonder if Sanderson had been in the Army.

In the chest of drawers in the bedroom there were some papers. So the man really had lived here. Electricity bills. Invoices for heating oil. Not much else, though. And nothing truly personal. No banking stuff – statements, cheque books or credit card bills. That was odd, too. He must have had some, somewhere.

Jake smiled ruefully. Perhaps Sanderson had kept stuff like that in his vehicle, as he tended to do himself, so as to be ready to move out quickly.

He returned to the kitchen and hunted in the rubbish bin until he found a clean, empty plastic bread bag. He slipped it on to his right hand like a glove and returned to the bedroom. There, he opened the wardrobe, one-handed. Sanderson hadn't been much of a dresser; there was very little there. A navy-blue, three-piece suit hung from the rail, with a white shirt and navy-with-red-dots tie tucked inside it. Sanderson's formal wear, it looked like. A green, waxed jacket was on another hanger. A pair of outdoor trousers on a third. On a shelf he saw two checked, flannel shirts, both well-worn. They had been washed and ironed. He poked at a collar until he could read the writing on the inside. 'Large' size, like the white shirt.

The next shelf held a few pairs of white underpants, waist-size medium, and also several pairs of short, woollen, grey socks, balled together in pairs.

A pair of size 10 black brogues, well polished, stood on the floor of the wardrobe.

Jake stood and considered. It was all neat and tidy, what there was of it, but there was so little. There must be other stuff somewhere – possibly in store. This place seemed to be no more than a temporary abode.

Then again, was his own place much different? Some people spent their whole lives just passing through. They didn't need or want anything else. Possessions wearied them. Made unnecessary clutter. Slowed or tied them down.

He shook his head and wondered how old Sanderson had been, but concluded only that he had been neither young nor old; not early twenties, judging by the lack of young-people stuff, no poster art or CDs. No fashionable gear. He couldn't have been elderly either. There were no spare spectacles lying about, nor slippers and no accumulation of knick-knacks. He'd probably been a self-contained, young middle-aged sort of man. Like himself, as someone had pointed out so recently, he thought wryly.

He re-checked the trousers hanging from the rail. They were medium length and had a thirty-eight waist. Sanderson had been quite a big man – tall, but not fat, certainly not heavy. Just over six feet, Jake guessed. And probably in good enough shape physically. If he hadn't been, it was unlikely he would have been living out here in such a remote location.

That raised the question of what he was doing here. Retired? Between things – jobs or wives, for instance? He hadn't been here long, anyway, and it looked temporary. A man living here permanently, or intending to, would have had more gear with him.

Perhaps the answer lay in the fact that someone had come looking for him – and had found him. Perhaps he'd been in hiding? For some reason, he'd had to drop everything and run. He'd been seeking a safe retreat, but in the end he hadn't managed to find one.

It was a thought that gave Jake reason to wince and pause. He could so easily imagine what it would have been like.

He wondered again about the coincidence of the hit on Sanderson and the attempted one on himself. Surely there couldn't be a connection between them? Surely not? But, now more than ever, he felt there might be.

He shook his head and moved on. No point speculating. He had to find some facts.

He returned to the living-room and studied the print on the wall, but was little wiser. It could have been anywhere, anywhere between North Africa and the North West Frontier. Still, it left him wondering if Sanderson had chosen it purely for aesthetic reasons or because he'd been there and seen it. It wasn't much, but it was a personal touch, a desert scene in a home that was itself virtually a desert.

That was about it for discoveries, apart from a toothbrush and other toilet equipment in the bathroom. There was nothing else. Not much of a footprint. Sanderson had lived lightly and left little behind.

Jake stood in silent contemplation for a moment. The guy had lived here a couple of years, they said, and this was all he had accumulated? What sort of life had it been? He shook his head. Even his own cottage had more in it than this one.

On his way to the front door, he passed the bathroom again. He stopped, went back inside and opened a wall cupboard he had not noticed before. The door swung open and he stared with surprise. The cupboard contained a shed-load of pills and tablets, and bottles and tubes.

He reached out with his still bag-gloved hand to move things around gently. He peered at the labels. It was quite a collection and not recreational either. All these were medicinal. Prescription drugs, mostly. Some of the names he knew. Others were a mystery, but they added up to one thing. Unless Sanderson was a world-champion hypochondriac, he'd been a very depressed, sleepless, anxious, troubled kind of guy.

And he'd been living out of a suitcase.

Why would Special Branch be interested in his death?

CHAPTER TWELVE

He met Dixie that evening in a pub up the valley, nearly twenty miles from Cragley. Jake was there first. He was studying the bar-meal menu when Dixie arrived. She slid on to the bench on the other side of the table and smiled.

'Jake.'

'Dixie!'

'We eating?'

'Might as well.' He pushed the menu across the table to her. 'How's it going?'

'Pretty good.' She scanned the menu in five seconds flat and said, 'Rainbow Trout and salad, please. No fries.'

'Drink?'

'Still water.'

He got up and went to the bar to order.

He smiled to himself. Dixie! Still the consummate professional. Did nothing that might impair her performance in the field. Ate and drank nothing she didn't need, or that carried a scent that might betray her. He was a long way past that level of dedication himself, if he'd ever had it, but he could still appreciate it.

'I like your little cottage,' she said when he sat down again.

'Oh? Seen it, have you?'

She nodded. 'It's a good place to hide out.'

'I'm not hiding out, Dixie.'

'No, of course you're not.'

She grinned at him. He scowled back but couldn't help thinking she looked great. So fit and healthy. She wore a tight black T-shirt under the brown field jacket. Neither did much to disguise the contours of her body. She looked in great shape.

She knew what he was looking at. Smiling, she slid the jacket off her shoulders. 'That better?' she asked mischievously.

He grinned and ducked his head. 'Sorry. Was I staring?'

'Just a bit.'

'Sorry.'

'I don't mind, Jake. Really.'

They made eye contact again and looked at each other seriously. Jake nodded and smiled again. Nothing had changed.

Their meals arrived. 'It's hot,' the waitress advised, as she placed Jake's steaming plate of lamb casserole before him. He was glad of the distraction.

'So what have you seen?' he asked when they were alone again. 'Anything?'

'Plenty. There's definitely something going on around the village.'

'I know that, Dixie.'

'I don't know yet what it is, though.'

She'd only had twenty-four hours. Still. . . .

Dixie developed a puzzled, thoughtful look. 'There are some people around, Jake, who I wouldn't have expected to find here.'

'That right?'

'Guys just looking, not at anything in particular. There's a woman, as well.'

He nodded. 'Tall, slim, thirty-ish? Long, blonde hair?'

'That's her.'

'She's the one I told you about. She knows my name, but she didn't do the shooting.'

'She didn't do the dying either. I've seen her today.'

'Where? I've been looking for her.'

Dixie shrugged. 'Around. A couple of places.'

Jake stood up and went to collect two coffees from the bar.

'What else?' he asked when he returned.

'I'm really not sure. There're people in the village just hanging about. Something's going to happen, but I don't know what yet.'

'They're planning something? What? Hit the bank?'

'You wouldn't bother planning that, surely? A country bank? You'd go straight in and out. Cash demand over the counter. Shotgun pointing at the teller. That would be enough.'

He nodded. That seemed about right.

'How many people have you spotted?'

'Three or four in the village. There're also people outside the village, scoping the countryside. One or two, at least. I keep picking up their trail.'

'Watching my place?'

'Sometimes. Watching the village, too.'

'That's a lot of people,' he murmured thoughtfully, wondering how he'd missed them all.

Dixie nodded.

It didn't make much sense. None of it did. Not from the very beginning.

'I'm pretty sure now I've not been the only target,' he said. 'In fact, I'm damn near certain.'

He went on to tell her what he'd learned at Fellside Farm.

Dixie listened, thought about it and then said, 'The guy – Sanderson – was hiding out there?'

He shrugged. 'Maybe.'

'He sounds a bit like you, Jake,' she said with a smile.

He grimaced, recalling again that Will Taylor had said something similar. It wasn't a comforting thought.

'Except I'm not hiding out, Dixie. And I'm not anxious, depressed or insomniac either. At least,' he added with a rueful grin, 'I wasn't.'

'Until the shooting started.'

He nodded. 'Until the shooting started.'

'So who was Mr Sanderson?' Dixie asked thoughtfully.

Jake nodded again. It was a good question, a very good question.

'Somebody has bracketed you together,' she added. 'Unless they made a mistake, there has to be a connection between you.'

'It's not possible,' he said slowly.

'You mean you don't want it to be?'

He just looked at her.

CHAPTER THIRTEEN

Jake had a nightcap with Tom when he got back to the hotel. It was getting to be a habit, he thought ruefully. He'd have scotch in his blood if he stayed here much longer.

'Anything more on the accident?' he asked.

Tom shook his head. 'Not that I've heard. He was shot, though, that fellow, Sanderson. There's no doubt about that. It'll all come out in the end, I expect. There'll have been all sorts of goings-on.'

Jake nodded. He leaned on the bar and waited to hear more, but Tom seemed tired. It was the tail-end of the evening, after a long day. The place was quiet, winding down to lights-out. The conversation was desultory, what there was of it – a companionable silence mostly.

A small television mounted on a wall was on, showing pictures but with no sound. It was a news programme. There were people in suits in front of a camera, studio scenes and arguments. Well, debates, at least.

'Isn't that our MP, the new Prime Minister?' Jake asked.

Tom peered hard at the screen and nodded. 'Fairly new. Since last year. Do you want to hear him?'

Tom's hand strayed towards a remote control device. Jake shook his head without much interest. 'Not now. I'm too tired.'

'You and me both. He's all right, though, MacGregor. It needs a Scotsman, even one down here, to argue the case for holding the country together. It's no good an Englishman doing that, not the way some of them fellows north of the border see it.'

That was probably right, Jake thought. 'Well, he's got the right constituency for it,' he said.

'Berwick? I'll say. It makes a change, having a Prime Minister from this part of the world.'

'What do you mean? Ramsay MacDonald was from the Borders, wasn't he? And Lord Home?'

'The Scottish side, though,' Tom pointed out, as if that settled the matter.

Jake yawned and gave up. He didn't have the energy for it. His eyes ranged over the bottles on the shelf behind the bar: whisky and whiskey, Scotch and rye, and corn. There were fancy bottles with exotic labels, showing coconut palms and pictures of blue seas; fierce rums; ice-like vodka and novelty alcohols he'd never heard of.

'Sell much of that stuff?' he asked.

Tom glanced over his shoulder and shook his head. 'Just at Christmas. Christmas and New Year. And funerals.'

'Not weddings?'

'They don't come here for weddings any more. They go to posh places. Five-star hotels in the Dominican Republic, and where have you, for a wedding on the beach. It costs them thousands, but they have the money, these days. Not like when we were young.'

Jake nodded without really listening. His eyes and thoughts moved on. He noted somebody had been asking recently for something other than beer or lager. There was a lemon on a wooden chopping board. Slices had gone from it. The knife was still in place. Juice glistened on the stainless steel blade.

'Gin and tonic?' he murmured absently.

Tom followed his eyes. 'Aye. That's what she wanted.'

Jake nodded. Then he looked round. There were the two of them, and there were two young lads in the bar.

'Who did?' Jake asked.

'That woman. The one that was here the other day.'

Jake's interest quickened. 'The blonde? She's back?'

Tom nodded and grinned. 'That's three guests in residence now. Almost a record.'

'You need extra staff.'

'That'll be the day!'

Tom snorted with derision and turned to head down the steps to the cellar.

So she was back, Jake thought, intrigued. What did that mean? Only one way to find out. He scanned the key board behind the bar. Old-fashioned keys here, not fancy electronic cards. The key to Number Two was missing now.

He stepped behind the bar and took the bunch of master keys from its hook. Each key was labelled with a plastic tag. He slid the one for Number Two off the ring and returned the bunch to its hook.

'I'm turning in,' he announced when Tom came up from the cellar. 'See you in the morning.'

'Aye. I'm hoping for an early night myself, if I can get rid of these two.' He nodded towards the corner where the two young lads were struggling to finish pints long since gone flat. 'You'd think they had no homes to go to.'

Jake grinned and left him to it. Back in his room, he read the previous week's local paper again. Then he read the safety notices on the wall and the tourist leaflets provided for guests. He skimmed information on walks and castles, ruins and churches and the legends of Cragley. He wondered how Dixie was getting on, and Apache, and he wondered what had been wrong with Cedric. He thought about the man who had died in his vehicle near Fellside Farm, and about the Sergeant's weary, despondent spirit. He thought about just about every damned thing he could think of.

At last he heard the church clock strike one. It was time.

It was impossible to move along the corridor silently, but he did his best. Already he knew the floorboards to avoid for big squeaks and loud creaks. He reached the door to Number Two, and paused. He put his ear to the door and listened. Nothing. Not a sound.

With great care, he slid the master key into the lock, relieved to find that there was no key on the inside to stop it.

He began to apply steady, gentle pressure to turn the key. It moved slowly, silently. He kept the pressure on, kept turning. The key sped the last quarter of its turn faster, and came to a stop. He tried twisting again but it would go no further.

He turned his attention to the handle, an old-fashioned, round, white porcelain handle that must have been in place for many years. It was loose in its housing which made it hard to avoid making a rattling noise. He took care. The handle turned smoothly enough. No squeak or squeal. It reached a stop. He kept the pressure full on and gently leaned against the door, willing it to open without a sound. It did. So far, so good.

He opened the door a little way, until there was enough of a gap for him to slip through. Then he closed the door carefully behind him and stood still, waiting for his eyes to adjust to the faint light seeping through the curtains from the sodium street lamp outside the hotel.

As his vision improved, he noted the position of the various pieces of furniture. The room was pretty much the same as his, except the bed was a single, instead of a double. It was pushed up against the wall. He began to move towards it, slowly, cautiously, patiently.

He reached the side of the bed and studied the long shape lying there. She was on her back. He could see her head and the white blur of her face. That made it easier. He had the surprise he'd wanted. Now he wanted her to wake, but quietly.

He leaned forward and gently but firmly pressed a hand over her mouth.

Simultaneously, something hard jabbed painfully into his lower ribs. He gasped and froze. His eyes flickered down to catch the gleam of metal. The light was too poor to see what make it was, but it was definitely a gun.

He removed his hand from her mouth.

'Check!' she said.

CHAPTER FOURTEEN

The bedside lamp came on. He slowly straightened up, watching her warily, unsure how this would go.

'I must be getting slow,' he suggested in as even a tone as he could muster.

'And noisy,' she said. 'Sit down, why don't you?'

She seemed unperturbed, relaxed even. He was relieved. She could have screamed. She could have pulled the trigger first and found out later who he was.

He sat on an old bentwood chair in front of a small dressing table. She tossed her quilt aside and sat up. Then she swung bare legs over the side of the bed and planted them on the floor. She gazed steadily at him all the while. The gun in her hand did, too. He could see now it was a Glock 17. Standard issue almost everywhere. And very deadly.

She was dressed in a voluminous white T-shirt that must have been XXXL, if not bigger. It hung around her in loose folds. Except at the front, where it clung provocatively to the swell of her breasts. He could see big dark nipples pressing hard against the thin cotton. He didn't want to but he couldn't help staring.

'Were you planning on raping me?' she asked with evident amusement at his discomfiture.

He shook his head and sighed. He tried to relax. 'I'm looking for information.'

'Not tempted even in the slightest?' she asked, head coquettishly to one side.

'Lady, that never entered my head!'

'And now. . . ?'

She arched her back, displaying her breasts to even greater advantage, and yawned. The gun pointed at the ceiling now. He smiled at last and chuckled.

She laid the gun down on the bed beside her. 'So what's the information you want?' she asked, playtime over.

'You knew my name,' he said. 'For a start, how did you find that out?'

'I got it from Central Records. I sent them a photo I took on my camera phone.'

'So you're in the Service?'

She didn't answer. She just smiled.

'You took a photo of me? Why?'

'You seemed to be watching me. I wondered if there was a reason.'

'Apart from. . . ?' he asked with a grin.

'Apart from the obvious, yes.'

'So you're in the Service?' he repeated.

'My lips are sealed.'

'And you discovered I used to be, too?'

She didn't reply directly. Instead, she asked, 'Do you fancy a coffee?'

He nodded. 'That would be civilized. So I'm Jake Ord. And you are?'

'Anna Mason.'

'And how long have you known my name?'

'A couple of days. Since I checked.'

She sighed then and shrugged. 'Speaking to you was a mistake, I'm afraid. I should have kept my big mouth shut, but I couldn't resist.'

A beginner, he thought. She was showing off – not been doing this for very long. A year or two, at most. And even less time in the field.

'So what's going on?' he asked.

She looked surprised. 'You mean you don't know?'

He shook his head.

'You've really been out of it, haven't you?' She reached for a folded newspaper on the bedside table and tossed it across to him. It was the local weekly. 'That's this week's edition, by the way.'

He took hold and unfolded it.

'Front page,' she added.

And there it was. The country's favourite prince, heir to the throne, was to visit Cragley soon to open a new social housing project.

He read the whole article. It took him a half minute.

'Next Friday,' he said. 'So you're. . . ?'

'Checking things out. Background stuff. Potential security threats. That sort of thing. That's what's going on,' she finished.

'That may be some of it,' he conceded. 'But that's not what the Service usually does,' he added, puzzled. 'What about Five, and the Met? Not to mention the local police?'

He wondered if there could be a terrorism connection to explain it. Anything seemed possible these days.

'Oh, they'll probably all be here,' Anna said airily. 'Actually,' she added, 'I could be Five, not Six. Have you thought of that?'

'You shouldn't be telling me,' he said with a smile. 'You shouldn't be telling anyone.'

'Maybe I lied?'

He chuckled. He suspected she was in the wrong job but he couldn't help liking her.

He was still puzzled, though. All this sounded like over-kill for a modest event in Cragley. Then he wondered if it was being used as a training exercise. That seemed quite likely, at least as far as Anna was concerned.

It didn't account for the attack on him, though, or the hit on Sanderson. There was more going on here than she might have realized.

'You're not alone, presumably?'

She shook her head. 'The preparations for this visit have been going on for some time, obviously. I'm sure you can guess how it's been.'

He could. Anna wasn't real security; she was background research. Perhaps they were just trying her out, testing her, giving her experience in the field. All new operatives had to start somewhere.

The electric kettle began to grumble. She stood up. Very tall, he was reminded. And wonderful legs, thighs as well as calves, now revealed in most of their glory.

She crossed to the little table and switched off the kettle. He watched as she ripped open two sachets of coffee and poured the contents into two cups.

'Milk?'

'Please.'

He watched her fiddle with two miniature containers. They yielded to her thumb nail, but not without trying her patience first.

'Damn things!' she muttered. 'Sugar?'

He shook his head.

'What are you smiling about?' she demanded, turning round and seeing the expression on his face.

'Nothing! Nothing at all. Honest.'

They grinned at one another. Then she shook her head and came to hand him his cup.

He held his breath as she came close, trying not to breathe in her scent, trying to stay focussed. It took a lot of effort.

'Relax!' she advised. 'I'm not going to eat you.'

'Or shoot me?'

She grinned again and sat back down.

'So how does it look?' he asked, trying to get back to business.

She shrugged. 'Not bad. You can't abolish risk, but a little place like this is as safe as anywhere. The police will put up temporary barriers and keep everyone on the far side of the road. No-one dangerous is going to get close. Besides, this isn't a high-risk function anyway. I mean, it's not political, or anything, is it?'

'No.'

It wasn't. Cutting the tape on an affordable housing project? Not political at all. People against war or missile systems, or global capitalism or global warming, would have better things to do than come here. Better opportunities than this, as well, to get their views on the front pages and into the main news bulletins.

On the other hand . . . The removable barriers would keep the crowds back, if there were any crowds, but they wouldn't stop bullets. And a sniper didn't need much in the way of facilities. All he needed was an opportunity and a motive.

Surely it wouldn't come to that though? Surely it was just coincidence that someone had been shooting at him shortly before a Royal visit?

And Sanderson. Not forgetting him.

'Where do I come in?' he asked.

'You?' She looked surprised for a moment. Then she smiled. 'You don't come into it at all, Jake. Or you wouldn't have, if I hadn't felt the need to show off by letting you know I'd identified you.'

He stared at her.

'You were watching me,' she added. 'It might have been just because you fancied me, but I needed to be sure. Leave no stone unturned. I needed to know who you were. So I found out.'

He shrugged and gave her a reluctant smile. 'So you didn't know who I was?'

'Not to begin with, no.'

'No-one told you in advance?'

She shook her head.

He supposed that was good. The Service hadn't been keeping tabs on him. They didn't know he was here. They hadn't been interested, which was understandable as well as a good thing. They were far too busy. They were stretched beyond reason by problems they hadn't known existed five or ten years ago.

'You seem puzzled,' she suggested. 'Are you disappointed I had no idea who you were?'

He shook his head. 'Relieved, if anything.'

He drained his coffee cup while he considered what to say next. A Royal visit explained Anna's appearance on the scene, but something else was going on as well. And he had to wonder if there was a connection. The attacks on him and Sanderson surely couldn't be coincidental? It was a lot to be happening in one small place, where normally nothing much at all ever happened.

'So here you are,' she suggested, stifling a yawn politely with the back of her hand, 'living in richly deserved, if far too early, retirement in this idyllic village. Then I turn up to remind you of the world of work.'

He smiled.

'Are you really living in retirement, by the way? You seem far too young for that. What on earth do you do all day?'

That was enough of that.

'There's a lot going on at the moment,' he said crisply. 'I don't think you know the half of it.'

'Oh?'

'A man living in seclusion not five miles away was killed the other day. Killed, not died.'

'Clive Sanderson.'

He looked at her sharply.

'Another one of yours,' she added. 'Another Old Boy from the … Service.'

Jake nodded thoughtfully. So he and Dixie had been on the right track with their suspicions. There was a connection between himself and Sanderson, even if he hadn't known what it was.

'What was he doing here?'

'Living in retirement. Like yourself.'

'Crap!'

'It's the truth, though. He'd been here eighteen months, or so.'

'Strange coincidence.'

'If you go somewhere remote, what can you expect?' she said lightly. 'You find anonymity best in big cities.'

'That's true.' He gave her a wry smile. 'But I didn't know him, Sanderson, that is. I'd never met him. Didn't even know he existed.'

'It's a big country, Jake.'

'You're starting to irritate me. Do you know that?'

She laughed. He liked it when she did that.

'What else?' she asked. 'Tell me something I don't know.'

'Try this. Whoever killed Sanderson tried to make it look like an accident.'

'So we hear.'

'Special Branch?'

She shrugged. 'What else?'

He took a deep breath, but now was the time.

'Sanderson wasn't the only target. Someone has had a go at me, as well. Twice. Twice that I know about. Three times, in fact,' he added, remembering Majorca.

She fell quiet and stayed quiet while he gave her an abridged version of events, notably missing out Dixie and his own snapping of someone's neck.

'You should have said earlier,' she told him curtly.

'I was dealing with it in my own way, but the Royal visit puts things into a different perspective. There's too much going on now and it may not be just a personal problem.'

She got to her feet.

'What now?' he asked.

'You'd better leave,' she said. 'I need to make a call.'

'Shooters,' he said, getting to his feet. 'Snipers. I'd have your people check possible sniper posts. In fact, I'd cancel the bloody visit!'

She didn't say another word. As he left, he wondered if he'd done the right thing or merely added another layer of confusion.

CHAPTER FIFTEEN

Anna didn't show up the next morning. Jake waited patiently. He had a long breakfast. He chatted to Maisie. He watched Maisie working, clearing the tables and re-setting them for the lunch trade. He took his coffee through to the bar, where he watched Tom removing glasses from the dishwasher. And he counted the bottles of scotch and fancy spirits hanging from their dispensers above the barman's shelf. Twenty-three. All waiting for Christmas and New Year. Or a funeral, and a wake.

He went out, wandered around the village and bought a paper. When he returned to the King's Arms, he saw a group of elderly people come in and sit down, and watched Maisie serve them egg-and-chips. No nonsense about salads for them, he noted. Too late now, probably, to worry about cholesterol levels.

Tom called, 'Waiting for someone?'

'No,' Jake said, shaking his head. 'Not waiting for anyone.'

Then he started looking seriously for Anna.

She wasn't in her room. In fact, it looked empty, as if she'd checked out. That worried him. He grimaced and left, wondering what it meant.

There was no sign of her in Main Street. He walked the length of it, and back again. He paused for a while and watched workmen putting the finishing touches to the new low-cost social housing scheme, due to be opened officially in a few days' time by the heir to the throne.

He wondered if Prince Charles would bring his wife with him. Probably, for the company. Not his sons, though. They had their own lives now. Too busy. God, he hoped so! He didn't want them here as well.

Two targets were enough. In fact, one was enough, more than enough.

Perhaps he was wrong? Maybe they wouldn't be targets at all. He could hope. Hope for the best, and plan for the worst. The old maxim still made sense.

He wandered back along Main Street. A car stopped outside the Heather View Guest House. The driver got out. It was Anna. He hurried to meet her.

'Busy?'

She turned towards him and frowned. 'Yes,' she said. 'Very.'

She reached inside the car and pulled out a briefcase.

'I assumed we would meet this morning?' he said.

She turned again and studied him. 'No point,' she said. 'Not after what I've heard. No point at all now.'

He stared at her. She seemed serious. He wondered what she meant.

'What did they say?'

She shook her head and turned to collect something else from the car.

'Anna!'

She looked round at him and shrugged. 'They said to keep away from you, for a start and that it was all rubbish, what you'd said. They said to keep away from you and get on with the job I'd been given, or they would find someone who would.'

'They said all that?'

He was surprised, shocked even, that his stock had fallen so low.

'And more!'

It made no sense. This was not what he'd expected to hear.

'Who're "they"?'

She looked at him and shrugged. 'My boss, essentially.'

'Who is?'

'Nothing to do with you, Jake. You're out of it – remember? Retired. Now go away, and let me get on with my job.'

One or two thoughts, and words, flew through his mind, but this was not the time to give voice to them.

'So I'm *persona non grata*?'

'Excuse me. I've got a lot to do.'

She slammed the car door shut and started towards the entrance to the guest house. It looked as though she'd found another base.

'What about the sniper shooting at me?'

'Police business – if it really happened,' she said over her shoulder. 'Nothing to do with us. We're not interested.'

'If it really happened? You can come and see the damage any time,' he said angrily. 'A guided tour!'

She didn't reply and she didn't look back.

Shit!

Jake's growing, nightmare suspicion was that all these things that had been happening were related. It might not be only a Royal visit in prospect; it might be a Royal assassination.

Obviously Anna's boss hadn't seen it that way.

So only Dixie and he knew the security people weren't the only army in the field. No-one else was trying to do anything about it either. And the clock was ticking, time was running out. Three days left? Less. It was three-and-a-bit now.

He found a seat under one of the huge horse chestnuts that dominated the village green. He could never remember the Latin name, damned fine trees, though. A hundred years old. More, probably. There were big creamy flowers on them in early summer and big, black rooks gathered in their branches all the year round. He watched a couple of rooks mob an intruding seagull that had come upriver with the tide, and he felt at one with them.

His mind returned to the possibility of a Royal assassination plot. If he had been given the job, how would he go about it?

On the far side of the green there was a parade of shops overlooking the housing project. There were possibilities there for a sniper and plenty of them. Any upstairs window might furnish a clear line of sight. He shook his head. It was too easy. He'd just put a man up there with a rifle. He wouldn't even have to be good. Just fair-ground competent. And with the balls and motivation to do it.

Crack! One shot should do it, and then another two or three to make sure. Easy pickings.

Then the shooter slips away; out of the building; out of the village. Not by the main road, though, as within a couple of minutes anything moving on the roads would be seen and challenged. There would be a helicopter somewhere overhead and patrol cars waiting in the wings to intercept.

Some other way. The shooter wouldn't have to go anywhere at all, of course. Not immediately. He, or she, could wait till the fuss died down. He didn't even have to be a visitor, although he probably would be.

But anyone staying here would be checked out. Anybody staying at any of the pubs, the handful of guest houses or the holiday cottages or rental flats. The police uniforms would do the rounds.

And day trippers would be registered at the check-points.

It would be difficult; easy to make the hit, but getting away afterwards would be the hard part.

He walked over to the library, and consulted a local 1:25,000 OS map in the reference section. He studied the farm tracks in the area. There were plenty of them, but most could be ruled out as escape routes because they led nowhere.

Stay put, then? Hole up in a farm or an isolated cottage. Possible, but unlikely. The district was sparsely populated. A new face wouldn't get through a single day without being spotted by someone.

No. His feeling was still that the shooter would want to be well away from the scene as soon as possible. In and out fast. How, though?

Staring at the map, he noticed something he hadn't seen before. What if the shooter walked calmly up the track to the old quarry near his cottage?

Then do what the sniper who'd attacked him had done: go over the escarpment and across the moor, pick up a vehicle parked on the other side and exit to the north, miles away from Cragley. Then across to the A1 – and away.

Do exactly what the sniper had done! Why not? It might even be the same man doing it.

Maybe that was why he'd been targeted? Perhaps they'd had no idea at all who he was. They'd just seen the occupant of his cottage as a potential hindrance, and wanted him out of the way. That could explain the attacks on him.

But what about Sanderson? How did he fit in?

No answer came to mind. Perhaps that was an entirely separate event. Just a simple coincidence. He sighed and gave up.

CHAPTER SIXTEEN

It was partly Jake, she thought wearily as she sipped a cup of coffee; partly Jake Ord, and what he'd had to say, plus that other man's death – Clive Sanderson. Jake was right. There did seem to be a lot going on around this little village.

It was only partly Jake though. She was also puzzled by Ed Donaldson's response and attitude when she'd talked to him on the phone. Normally such a calm and thoughtful man – as good a boss as you could imagine – he'd been brusque with her, and quite savage about Jake.

'Nothing to do with you, Anna. Keep away from the man. Get on with your job.'

'But, Ed! There may be a connection, a security risk. I just think. . . .'

'He'll have invented it. Probably nothing at all has happened. Even if it has, it's nothing to do with us. And it's most certainly not why you are there. Keep your eye on the ball, Anna.'

After a second or two she had realized their brief conversation was over. The connection had been ended. She grimaced and switched off her phone.

She didn't like being ticked off as if she was some office junior or the cleaner, but she had to accept it. After all, he was the big boss, not just her line manager. She was lucky he'd taken an interest in her. No doubt he would have his reasons for what he'd said. Good reasons.

At first, she'd assumed Jake must have had a lot to answer for when he left the Service. But what on earth had he done?

She could find nothing. No-one she spoke to had even heard of Jake. And she had no access to the MI6 personnel records that might have told her. Anything big would surely have leaked out into her own department's grapevine and gathering places. Five always knew about shenanigans at Six, and no doubt vice-versa. Professional secret keepers were not that good at concealing secrets, especially scandals, from each other. They were like everybody else when it came to dishing the dirt.

Yet Ed had been so brutally uninterested in her tale of the attack on Jake, especially in the light of Sanderson's demise the same night, surely he should have been concerned? After all, it was former colleagues she was talking about. Did they count for nothing? At least he could have spoken to someone at the Met, or even the Northumbria Police, but no. He had just warned her to keep away from Jake, and that was that. He'd been indifferent to the suggestion that Jake was in continuing danger, and indifferent to the possibility of a link to the Prince's visit. In fact, he'd been in denial. That was what it came down to.

Afterwards she had driven over to Jake's cottage and seen the damage for herself. It was limited, but she could see he hadn't just made it up. The attack really had happened. Jake really was in danger. And so might the Prince be.

Now she wasn't sure what to think, or to do.

Never one to give up just because someone important didn't like him, Jake decided to have another go at Anna. He caught her coming out of the guest house.

'I don't want to get you into trouble,' he began.

'No, of course not.'

She continued walking towards her car. He followed.

'Presumably there's nothing I could say that would interest you in my point of view?'

'Nothing at all.'

'Absolutely nothing?'

'Absolutely.'

He sensed she was weakening.

'You could always look at my cottage,' he suggested. 'Or Sanderson's Jeep Cherokee, or whatever it was – if the local cops will let you anywhere near it.'

She stopped and opened the door of her car. 'What do you want, Jake?' she asked over her shoulder as she climbed inside.

'A photo of Sanderson.'

He turned away.

'Meet me in the King's Arms – or Head, or whatever it's called,' he heard her say quietly. 'Seven tonight.'

He didn't acknowledge her proposal. He was already walking away. He didn't stop, or even slow. She slammed the door shut

He headed casually back towards the green. As he went, he wondered where they were, the security people. Somewhere nearby, undoubtedly. Somewhere they could keep an eye on things, and on Anna.

The trouble was, if he was right, someone else was keeping an eye on them, too. There were bad guys monitoring the activities of the good guys. He wondered if the good guys knew.

His mobile vibrated in his pocket. He ducked under the awning in front of the greengrocer's before he took it out.

'Above the chemist's,' Dixie informed him, as if she'd been mind reading. 'That's where one of them is.'

'Whose side is he on?'

'Beats me. I'll see if I can find out.'

The phone went dead. Jake frowned. Someone above the chemist's shop would have had a good view of him approaching Anna. It would be interesting to hear if her boss got to hear of it. If he didn't, it meant whoever was above the chemist's was on the other team.

Whoever it was, they couldn't have made much of his encounter with Anna. She'd made it very visibly plain that she wouldn't talk to him. Clever girl! Now he'd have to wait and see if she could deliver.

She looked terrific when she entered the bar. Heads would definitely have turned, Jake thought, had there been anyone there but him. He managed to keep cool.

She sat down across the table from him.

'Drink?'

She shook her head and looked hard at him. 'Why did you want a photo?'

He shrugged and took a sip of his beer before answering. 'I'm not sure, to be honest. I just wondered if I did know him, after all. I don't remember the name, but maybe that doesn't mean much.'

She was still staring at him, still trying to pick out meaning, a hidden message.

'Have you ever been to the National Gallery of Modern Art in Edinburgh?' he asked.

She shook her head.

'Last time I was there, a big internal wall, two or three storeys high, was covered with names. Small, black writing on a vast white wall. Hundreds and hundreds of them. Very impressive. At first I assumed it was a war memorial of some sort – like the one at Arlington.'

'The Vietnam one?'

He nodded.

'And is it?'

'No. It's an exhibit, a work of art. The artist – I guess you can call him that – wrote down the names he could remember of everyone he'd ever met.'

'What for?'

'Because . . .' He shrugged. 'It's just art, modern art. Or should I say "contemporary art"?'

'I see.' She nodded thoughtfully. 'Everyone you ever met? You couldn't possibly remember them all, could you?'

'No. I think he just wanted to see how many he could remember.'

She thought about that some more. 'You might have forgotten Sanderson?' she suggested.

'I might, yes.'

'Maybe I will have a drink, after all. Fresh orange and tonic, please. With whisky in it.'

He grinned and set off to roust Tom from his slumbers behind the bar.

'It's not a very good picture, I'm afraid,' she volunteered when he returned. 'Can you see it?'

'Just about.'

He took the phone from her and studied the screen. The image was very grainy and a bit blurred.

'Mobile phones are very useful,' she added, 'but their camera work is in its infancy. At least, on mine it is. The later models are a lot better.'

He ignored all that. He was concentrating.

'Do you recognize him?'

He studied the picture on the little screen some more. He stared at it hard.

'I can see if I can get it printed, if that would help?' she suggested. 'Or put it up on a monitor somewhere. The library maybe?'

'There's an internet café in the village.'

'Is there? Even better. We can go there.'

'No,' he said, shaking his head. 'There's no need.'

'You don't remember him?' she said with disappointment.

'On the contrary,' he said slowly. 'I remember him very well.' He looked up at her and added, 'But I knew him as Doug Kennedy.'

'Oh?' she said, gazing at him thoughtfully. 'That's interesting.'

'Isn't it?'

'The way I see it,' Jake said carefully, 'is that the Prince would make a splendid target.'

They were outside now. Anna turned round. She looked up and down the main street and nodded agreement. 'For a sniper,' she said.

'For any half-decent shot. He doesn't have to be an expensively trained, professional sniper.'

'How many windows would give him the opportunity?'

Jake didn't even look up. 'Two hundred? Not many more.'

She grimaced. He could see the thoughts racing through her head.

'You can't cover them all,' he pointed out gently.

'I never thought we could.'

'And you couldn't take the Prince in the back way either. He's going to be exposed if he comes. In fact, he probably wouldn't come if he couldn't be. They do it at least partly for the exposure, the publicity.'

'But the Royal family don't expect to be shot at,' she pointed out tartly.

'No, that's not part of the deal.'

'We need to start checking,' she said dubiously. 'See who's in the flats behind the windows.'

'They're not all flats. Some are just store rooms above the shops.'

'There are still a lot of windows. We'll have to get the local police on to it.'

He wasn't sure. The police could be good at jobs like that, but . . . Would the local men know what they were looking for?

'You could cut the workload down a bit. A lot of the accommodation is holiday flats. Concentrate on them first.'

She nodded agreement. 'I'll get them started.'

'What would they be looking for?'

'Single men. Or women. The sniper doesn't have to be a man.'

'Doesn't have to be single either. Could be a team.'

That stopped her. She shook her head. 'So what do you suggest?'

'Get the police doing the rounds, by all means – if they've got the manpower. Seeing who's there. Making lists. Looking for things that don't add up.'

'But?'

'But my hunch is we might get lucky by focussing on specific buildings. The shooter is going to want to get out fast and unnoticed. Some of those buildings have discreet entrances at the back. One of them would be ideal.'

She nodded. 'I'll mention it. Then, perhaps, you and I could have a look around?'

'It might get you into trouble – more trouble.'

'I'll deal with it, if it does.'

Good for you! he thought, but he didn't say anything.

It was a start, he thought then, encouraged, but no more than that. He didn't hold out a lot of hope. They were trying to find a way into what could be a very well-laid plan.

'Tell me,' he said thoughtfully, 'just who is responsible for security these days?'

She looked at him.

'Someone's got a big job,' he pointed out gently. 'Who is it?'

CHAPTER SEVENTEEN

There had been a lot of re-structuring of the various security organizations in recent years, much of it driven by concerns about terrorism. Listening to Anna describe the current arrangements, Jake almost wished he'd paid more attention at the time the changes had been announced. Almost. It wasn't his world any more though.

'So the local Special Branch will still be involved?' he asked.

'Oh, yes. You've got to have the local police involved. No Chief Constable would willingly surrender all responsibility for what happens on his patch.'

'But the major player is "Royalty Protection" from this "Protection Command"?'

'Which is part of Specialist Operations at the Met.'

'Jesus! How do they remember who they work for?'

'It's still the Metropolitan Police Service, just as it always was.'

'Just as it always was?'

She laughed and punched his arm. 'The same officers, probably. It's just that it's better organized now.'

'Do you really think so?'

'Jake, stop being a reactionary old git! This is the modern police service we're talking about. They can't stand still in the face of everything that's happening in the world.'

'True.' He nodded and tried to look wise. 'Very true. Let's hope all this re-structuring works, or works better.'

'I'm sure it will – does, I mean.'

Jake wished he shared her confidence. In his experience, one re-organization soon led to another, and another, which in turn often reversed previous changes. If the guy at the top got the idea he could do it, he usually did. Then he moved on, and his successor got the chance to put his own imprint on the structure. And so on, ad infinitum.

Or was he just being cynical? Probably.

'Do you know any of the Protection Command people?'

'Some.'

'Here, in Cragley?'

'Maybe. Why?'

'Is there anyone you could talk to, explain your fears to? Anyone who might take seriously what's been happening here, and the possibility of a Royal assassination attempt?'

She looked dubious. 'I could try, I suppose.'

'We have to find some way of bypassing your boss, even if it's just a matter of sowing seeds of doubt in the right ear.'

'You're right. I can't get anywhere with Ed. He's made extremely clear what his views are. I'll try. I have met someone in Specialist Protection.'

'What's that?'

'Another part of Protection Command. They look after the politicians, as opposed to Royalty.'

'Are they here, as well?'

She nodded. 'Apparently.'

He didn't bother asking why, but the word "superfluous" came to mind.

'Good,' he said heavily. 'And if you come across local Special Branch people, tell them, as well. The more that know, the better.'

She frowned, but didn't respond.

He knew it wouldn't be easy for her. Lines of command were kept well clear of each other in all serious organizations: one wouldn't interfere with another. It took a rare person, a maverick, a whistleblower even, to cross lines. He didn't know if Anna was such a person, but he hoped so. They had to try.

She glanced at her phone to see who was calling, and then took the call.

'What did I tell you?' the familiar voice asked without preamble.

'About what?' she asked cautiously.

'I told you to keep away from Ord. I thought I had made that very clear.'

She grimaced. He wasn't pleased.

'He does have legitimate grounds for concern, you know, Ed. He's not been making it up. And Sanderson—'

'None of that is our business. This is an active operation of the highest importance. Whatever trouble those two have got themselves into is not – I repeat not – our concern. That's what the police are for. Remember?'

'But they may be connected! That's the whole point—'

'You have your instructions, Anna. Follow them – to the letter.'

The phone went dead. She grimaced again. She couldn't understand it. What on earth was the problem? Surely it was right to follow up on things happening in the area?

Oh, she didn't understand this at all! What on earth was she to do? Use her initiative, as training had drummed into her, or just follow orders?

She sighed. Perhaps she did just have to buckle down and get on with it. She had to assume he knew what he was doing, and what he was talking about. She just had to. He wouldn't have got where he was if he'd been stupid or ineffective. Obviously she didn't have the full picture. For all she knew, the Department could have other people following up on Jake and Sanderson.

Yes, perhaps that was it, she thought hopefully. How stupid of her to imagine that because she wasn't to do it, no-one else was either.

Donaldson was feeling less charitable. That bloody woman! If he'd wanted someone to do some investigating, he wouldn't have sent her. The whole point of having her here was in danger of being undermined.

Well, not on his watch! The stakes were too high.

He glanced absently at the phone in his hand and switched it off. He felt like throwing it at the wall. Somehow he restrained himself and slipped it back into his pocket. Then he changed his mind, got it back out and rang his contact in Protection Command.

After that he rang Williams. Better to sort it all out in one go.

'We're going to have to do it,' he told Williams almost with regret. 'Take Grey with you. And keep it quiet.'

'Now?'

'As soon as you can. You know what to do.'

'Tonight would be best.'

'Whenever. You know what to do.'

'Mr Ord?'

Jake looked up from his coffee and nodded. The man looked official. Smart suit. Slim. Medium height and weight. Greying hair. He looked out of place in The King's Arms.

'Chief Superintendent Rob Grainger, Royal Protection Squad.'

'That's part of Protection Command at the Met these days, isn't it?'

'That's right. You're well informed.'

'I have a good informant.'

'So I understand,' Grainger said without a smile.

'Take a seat. Coffee?'

Grainger nodded and sat down. Jake waved at Maisie to fetch more coffee. She grabbed the pot from the coffee machine and hurried over.

'I don't know what it'll be like by now,' Maisie said. 'It's a long time since I made it.'

'It'll be fine,' Jake assured her.

Grainger concurred with a small smile. But he didn't touch the cup once Maisie was gone. Obviously used to a superior standard of coffee.

'How can I help you?' Jake asked, looking up at Grainger.

'What's your relationship with Miss Mason? Let's start there.'

Straight to the point, Jake noted. It suited him.

'I didn't know she even existed until the other day. I had some trouble …. She tell you?'

Grainger nodded.

'She was around, an obvious stranger. We got talking. That's it, really.'

Grainger nodded and stirred his coffee, eyeing it suspiciously. 'Got talking?'

'As I said, she was an obvious stranger. Suspicion flared.'

'You suspected her of . . . something?'

'Crazy, isn't it?'

'Normally, MI5 people are famous for being invisible.'

'That's what the public likes to think.'

'But you spotted her? Doing undercover work?'

'Amazing, isn't it?'

Grainger nodded. He was good, Jake decided. He was doing a nice, gentle job of sowing doubt and teasing out information. But he didn't warm to the man. And he wasn't interested in taking part in elaborate games with him.

'Look, let's get straight to it. Did she tell you what I used to do?'

'She did. But you're retired now?'

'That's right. So was Sanderson, the guy killed the other night.'

'I heard about that incident.'

'I bet you did! Your people are out at his cottage right now.'

'Not mine.'

'Colleagues from the Met, then.'

'Mr Sanderson's death is being investigated, yes.'

Grainger was giving absolutely nothing away. He'd come for information. That was all. Jake was becoming less and less impressed with his approach.

'Miss Mason says you believe there's a link to the Royal visit?'

'The possibility of a link.'

'Evidence?'

'None. But it's too much of a coincidence. Someone should be looking into it.'

'What makes you think they aren't?'

Jake sighed and shook his head. He took a sip of coffee before he answered.

'Look, Grainger. We could play this game all day. I'm tired of it. We – I, mostly – simply wanted you to be aware of what's been happening around here these last few days. It's up to you what you do with it.'

'Miss Mason isn't retired, is she?'

Jake stared at him.

'She reports to a superior officer, as we all do. And as you yourself must have done in the dim and distant past. Am I right?'

Jake waited. He couldn't believe the way this was going.

'Did Miss Mason tell you what her superior officer said when she reported her concerns and misgivings?'

Jake got to his feet. 'We're done here,' he said. 'And the coffee's paid for.'

'MI5 is another jurisdiction,' Grainger continued unperturbed, 'with their own management system, with which we do not interfere. I'm Royalty Protection.'

'So you said. I hope you're good at your job,' Jake said, looking down at him.

'Oh, I am! Make no mistake.'

'Then get on with it.'

He turned away and left, reasonably satisfied despite his irritation. Grainger had been given enough to get him started. If he really was any good, he would look into things now without Five being able to warn him off. It wasn't their exclusive territory. But he suspected Anna wouldn't be flavour of the month back at her office.

CHAPTER EIGHTEEN

Cops often looked different these days; smart casual instead of plain-clothes uniform, but they still came in twos, and they still had that unmistakable air of confident authority about them that came with knowing they had the Law on their side. Jake was in no doubt who they were as soon as they appeared, or who they had come to see. For a few moments, though, he was unsure why.

'Mr Ord?' the short, stubby, tough-looking one asked.

Jake nodded and gave him a pleasant smile.

'Mind if I sit down?'

'Not at all. If you're going to the bar, mine's a pint of Black Sheep. It has a nice, tangy taste to it.'

'Comedian!'

As he sat down, the newcomer flashed an identity badge. Jake could have asked to study it, but he didn't bother. He was sure enough who they were. Besides, he was curious to know what they wanted with him. A follow-up to Grainger's visit that afternoon, probably.

The younger of the two, taller but also heavily-built, sat down at a neighbouring table, keeping a deferential but watchful distance.

'DI Jack Collins,' the lead cop said across the table, 'Metropolitan Police. And DS Dave Evans.'

'You're a long way from home.'

'Aren't we?' Collins smiled and said in a quiet, conversational tone, 'We're not buying a drink, for you or for ourselves. In a minute we'd like you to come with us.'

'Because?'

'Because we'd like to talk to you about a few things.'

'Do it here.'

'It wouldn't be appropriate.'

'Here seems fine to me.'

Collins shook his head, leaned forward and said, 'A colleague believes you have certain . . . conspiracy theories. We'd like to talk to you about them, in confidence. With no risk of being overheard.'

Jake could guess the rest of it. Grainger had not been satisfied.

And, increasingly, it sounded as if Anna had not approached the right man in the first place. Either that or word had got back to her boss, as they should have anticipated. His fault. Not hers. He was the one with the experience. Now things were worse than before.

'Conspiracy theories?' he said mildly, wondering how much Collins knew.

Still smiling, Collins nodded and said, 'Are we ready to go?'

'Sure. How long will it take?'

'A few days. No more.'

Ah!

Definitely something to do with Anna's boss. Get him off the street for a while, boys. Out of the way.

Nice!

He could object. Refuse to go. Then what would they do? Arrest him for questioning about a suspected conspiracy? Take him into protective custody?

Whatever they did, it would have the same result. It would get him out of the way until whatever was going to happen had happened. The bad guys, whoever they were, would be laughing their socks off. Cops making their job easier!

'Do you want to hear my story?' he asked.

'Later,' Collins assured him. 'We'll have all the time in the world later. Finish your pint. Then let's go.'

'Where to?'

'A hotel of our choice.'

'Sounds nice. Do I need my solicitor?'

Collins merely smiled.

Jake shook his head. 'I need to get a few things from my room first.'

'You don't need a thing.'

'I do.' He was firm on that point. 'Come up with me. It won't take long.'

Collins hesitated, but only for a moment. Then he turned to his colleague. 'Bring the car round, Dave. We'll just be a couple of minutes.'

Dave nodded, stood up and headed for the door.

Collins followed Jake upstairs to his room. 'Nice,' he remarked, sniffing and looking round with fascination at the décor. 'Very nice!'

'Not bad, is it?' Jake responded.

He stuffed a tooth brush and one or two other things into a small plastic bag.

'It's like going on holiday in 1935,' Collins said.

Comedian. Jake laughed and moved into the bathroom.

'Leave the door open,' Collins called.

'Right!'

He shut the door anyway and slammed home the heavy brass bolt, made in an age when they used proper metal for bolts and proper wood for doors. Even as Collins hurled himself against the door the first time, Jake had the sash window open and was already halfway out.

He dropped the ten feet to the flat roof over the hotel kitchen and scrambled down into the lane beyond. Then he started jogging. He didn't stop until he reached the garage where he kept the elderly BMW.

The car started first go. Hopefully, he thought, as he turned out into the main road, although Collins might have someone watching his Land Rover, he wouldn't know about the car.

No-one tried to stop him as he headed west out of the village, making for open country.

CHAPTER NINETEEN

Dixie looked less pristine than usual. Mud on her trousers. Red-weathered face. Tough smile.

'How's it going?' Jake asked cautiously.

She shrugged. 'Nothing much to report.'

He nodded. 'Hungry?'

'Just a bit.'

He guessed she'd been extending herself. So he ordered some food and drinks and got them settled in a discreet corner of the near-empty bar before he raised business again. Gave her a chance to sort her thoughts out.

'I've found out part of what's going on in the village,' he said. 'And I've found out what Anna Mason – the blonde we wondered about – is doing. There's a Royal visit coming up in the next few days. The Prince of Wales. She's part of background security.'

'From MI5?'

'I think so. But I'm not sure. She might be from the Met, I suppose.'

'Why the Met?'

'They've done a lot of re-structuring in recent years. Beefed up the Royal Protection squad. She might be from there.'

Dixie nodded thoughtfully and stirred her drink. 'What's the visit about?'

'Official opening of a subsidized housing scheme for less well-off, or otherwise disadvantaged, people.'

'And they need the Prince of Wales to do that? The heir to the throne, isn't he?'

'The heir to the throne,' Jake agreed. 'He's coming to cut the tape. It's an opportunity for some good local publicity, I guess, and it gives him an excuse to get out of London for a day or two. He'll probably visit his relatives in Alnwick Castle for the weekend while he's here, I shouldn't wonder.'

'Can't blame him for that.' She rubbed her eyes, which looked as if they hadn't been closed for a long time. 'But how does that relate to what's going on with you?'

'I don't know. At first I couldn't see any connection at all, but now . . .' He hesitated and scratched his head. 'Now I'm beginning to wonder if there's going to be an attempt to assassinate him, and we're somehow caught up in it. Me and Sanderson. Maybe he's the main target, not us.'

He shrugged and broke off.

Dixie stared hard at him. 'And you and Sanderson became involved because. . . ?'

'Because of what he and I used to do for a living, presumably. Maybe we're thought to be in the way. Possible impediments.'

She nodded thoughtfully. 'Too much of a coincidence otherwise?'

He shrugged.

'It gets worse, Dixie. The police have just tried to take me into custody. So now I'm guilty of evading arrest – as well as everything else.'

She just looked at him.

He shrugged again. 'People seem to want me off the board, one way or another. Both sides, in fact. I'm getting a very bad feeling about all of this.'

'You do attract trouble, Jake, don't you?'

He grinned. 'Just like old times, eh?'

She grinned back. 'It's a good thing I'm here.'

He leaned forward and spoke with more urgency. 'We need to move things along faster, Dixie. I'm not getting anywhere much. And neither are you, from what you've said.'

'Not for want of trying, Jake.'

'I know that. Don't get me wrong. It's just that if I'm right we don't have a lot of time. The Royal visit is in three days' time.'

'Talk to the security people?'

'No point. Especially not now. They seem to think I'm part of the problem.' He shook his head. 'I gather from Anna that I'm *persona non grata* with them, for some unknown reason. She's been told to keep away from me. And they're not interested in what I have to say.'

'Why might that be?'

'Can't tell you. All I know is I appear to be regarded officially as a nuisance.'

'You Brits!' Dixie said, shaking her head and giving a weary chuckle. 'So what do you suggest we do?'

'I'm going to move back into the cottage. See what happens. If someone really does want me out of the way, that will give them an opportunity to try again.'

Dixie thought it through before she spoke again. 'I may not be able to give you the protection you need, Jake. And you're going to be awfully vulnerable, sitting there, waiting.'

'You got a better idea?'

She hesitated and then shook her head.

'Well, it's a risk I'm prepared to take,' Jake said. He paused and added, 'What I'm not prepared to do is sit around in a pub any longer just talking about it.'

'I remember the day when. . . .'

'I know. So do I!'

He looked at her and smiled. 'There isn't exactly an army out there, Dixie. There're . . . what? Two or three men on one side? Not many more.' He paused and added ruefully, 'Plus the Met and MI5 on the other side, of course.'

'And there're . . . what? Three of us?'

'Three?'

'Me, you and the Mason woman.'

He looked at her. 'You think she's on our side?'

'On your side, Jake. Yes, I do think that.'

He chuckled. But Dixie didn't.

Afterwards Jake found himself thinking about Doug Kennedy, and their time together. And Ellie, of course. It all seemed such a long time ago now. It was a long time ago. Sometimes he feared he would forget what Ellie looked like. Time could do that; time and the healing process. The human mind has ways of re-shaping the past to make the present more comfortable.

He could recall Doug Kennedy clearly enough though. No problem there: a big guy, quiet and conscientious, studious even. He was reliable – good in a tight corner.

They had worked together in one or two places in the Middle East. Helping HMG prop up governments and movements regarded as friendly. Protecting the oil supply. Keeping a lid on the fanatics wanting to spread death and destruction.

Then once he and Ellie had found themselves working together with Doug. They were out in the desert; miles from anywhere; miles from help – no Special Forces to call on in the event of things getting sticky.

The senior officer in charge on that operation had been a guy he hadn't much liked. Rogers, Will Rogers. A man with a big and growing reputation. Liked by his superiors because he got things done. Disliked by a lot of his colleagues because he took risks, cut corners. He had a reputation for getting people killed, as well as getting results.

The US had an interest, and a presence, too. So Jake had been sent out into the wilds with Dixie. It had been a futile, wild-goose chase. Totally unnecessary. They could have waited for the bad guys to come to them, instead of having to chase them round the desert. But that was Rogers's way; being pro-active; demonstrating action and initiative. Sometimes it worked.

Jake and Dixie had been OK. They had achieved nothing, but they had come back unscathed. When they got back, they'd found that Ellie and Doug Kennedy had not been so fortunate. Doug had been badly injured and airlifted to some distant hospital. Ellie was dead.

Explanation and regrets had not been anywhere near good enough.

They were all soldiers, Rogers had pointed out. They had taken the Queen's shilling – with a smiling apology to Dixie. The outcome was unfortunate. But that was life, and war. And it was war, of a kind.

Rogers was right, of course. He'd also been true to his reputation. That had rankled. But there had been nothing to be done.

Jake had quit in disgust and fury.

There was nothing to be done now either. He knew that. And he knew he had to stop going over old ground. Nothing would bring Ellie back, nor Doug Kennedy either.

CHAPTER TWENTY

He returned to Cragley under cover of darkness. He had things to do there. Things to collect. Besides, he figured Collins and company were probably all in bed by then. Royalty protection!

It was nice along by the river, quiet and still. Moonlight reflected off the water – a good place to wander and think. But not about Ellie. Ellie was then. This was now. He had current problems to address, and addressing them didn't come easily.

The first rustle might have been the wind. Except there wasn't any. He paused momentarily and then kept going, but now he was fully alert and listening hard. There it was again. Not much, but enough.

He stepped off the path between two hawthorn bushes. It was even quieter now, but someone was coming. He could hear a faint rustle as a moving body brushed against the grass to either side of the path. He flexed his shoulders and braced himself.

There was a blur of movement. Then a dog was sniffing at his feet. It bumped into him and sniffed harder at his leg and its tail started flopping about wildly.

'Jake? That you, Jake?' a voice said softly.

'Jesus Christ, Cedric! You scared the shit out of me.'

'Sorry.'

The familiar bulky shape of Cedric emerged out of the gloom. Rupert moved on, Jake a too familiar scent to detain him for long.

Jake wondered how Cedric had got so close without his being aware of it. He wasn't proud of himself.

'I saw you in the lane,' Cedric said with a chuckle. 'And I was coming this way myself.'

Very quietly, Jake thought. He wondered why. He also wondered if Cedric was in a better mood than last time they'd met. He decided to take it slowly.

'Nice night, Cedric.'

'Not bad. Walk with me, Jake. Come back to the house for coffee.'

Jake didn't reply immediately.

'I'm sorry about what I said before – last time we met,' Cedric added. 'I apologize.'

'Don't worry about it.'

'But I do. Come on.'

Jake hesitated a moment. Then he fell into step. He could ill afford the time but he wanted to give Cedric a fair hearing. Besides, he was curious. He sensed this was no casual encounter.

They strolled along the riverside for a couple of hundred yards. Jake was glad Rupert was out in front, sussing out anything that shouldn't be there. Rupert was a lot more useful as a companion than a cat, he thought wryly.

'How's Apache doing?'

'Taken to it as "to the manor born". Cat Heaven, down in that cellar.'

Jake smiled. Cedric seemed more himself. Something must have upset him the other morning. That was all. Maybe a pot hadn't turned out the way it should. Or it had cracked. It could happen.

They turned away from the river, turned inland towards the centre of the village.

'Coming back for that coffee, Jake?'

'A bit late for Caitlin, isn't it? I don't want to disturb her.'

'She's not here – gone to her sister's for a couple of days.'

'Has she? That's not like her.'

Caitlin never went anywhere without Cedric.

'No, well . . . She's not been herself lately. I felt she needed a change, a rest. So I suggested she went to see Shona.'

'Coffee sounds good, in that case.'

Cedric poured two mugs of coffee from the flask on the coffee maker. He put them on the table, sat down and stared at Jake. 'You're in trouble,' he said evenly. 'How can I help?'

Jake hesitated, but only for a moment. Time was pressing.

'I might need somewhere to stay, Cedric. Just for a couple of days. Tom's place is . . .' He grimaced. 'Well, it's just not safe for me at the moment.'

'Stay here, Jake. As long as you like.'

'There might be some trouble, Ced. Real trouble. It could follow me.'

'We'll deal with it, if it does.'

Jake thought about that. He wondered if he was about to bring death and destruction down on his friends. Cedric and Caitlin didn't deserve that. Could he justify the risk?

'We've known trouble before in our lives,' Cedric added.

'Not like this.'

'Probably exactly like this.'

'I don't think so.'

Cedric nodded. 'We've lived in some funny places, Jake, Caitlin and I. And we've seen some strange goings-on.'

Jake must have looked doubtful. Cedric stood up and beckoned to him. He led the way into an adjacent room. There, he opened a cupboard fixed to the wall. Behind it was a safe sunk into the wall. Cedric spun the numbers and opened the safe. He opened the door wide and stepped back, inviting Jake to look inside.

The safe contained several handguns and a number of boxes of ammunition.

Jake stared and shook his head. 'What the hell did the pair of you do before you took up art and antiques?'

'Don't ask,' Cedric advised with a chuckle. 'Stay as long as you like, Jake. Your lady friend, as well, if she wants.'

That was another surprise.

'You know about her?'

Cedric nodded. 'Oh, yes,' he said. 'Ain't nothing secret, is there? Not really.'

'He's here.'

'Good. Keep him there.'

'It might not be easy.'

'Just do it.'

He grimaced, put down the phone and returned to his visitor.

Cedric led Jake into another room, one he hadn't been in before. It had book-lined walls, a comfortable chair, and a desk. There were some reading lamps dotted about and a couple of pictures.

'My favourite room in the house,' Cedric said with satisfaction, pointing Jake to a chair.

'Your study, eh?'

Cedric chuckled. 'Hardly that. Coffee do you, or something stronger?'

'Coffee's fine, thanks.'

Cedric headed off back to the kitchen and Jake took this as an invitation to look around. Ordinarily they would both have been in the kitchen still. He headed for the book shelves, curious about a lot of things, not least Cedric himself now.

There was a lot of old stuff on the shelves. Very old, in some cases, ancient even. Some of it was much travelled, as well, with worn and battered leather bindings. There were thick, heavy books, small ones coming apart and loose folios, too. A few dealt directly with artistic and antiquarian subjects, but not many. A couple of shelves of books were in the Arabic language; that was a surprise.

He studied a small, framed water-colour of a desert scene. How curious to have such a thing here, in this world of moorland. He studied the letters in the bottom left-hand corner, and realised they formed Cedric's initials. That was another surprise – Cedric the painter. Or was it Caitlin?

He took a book from the shelf at random and blew gently on the top. No dust rose from it.

'Admiring the library?' Cedric said, coming back through the doorway.

'Quite a collection you've got. I didn't know about this . . . this hobby of yours.'

'I have to have something to occupy me. I can't be making coffee mugs with all my time.'

Evidently not.

Jake took one of the mugs of coffee and sat down with it. He looked around the room. 'You're certainly well established here, Cedric.'

'I would take some moving, wouldn't I?'

'How long have you been here?'

'Oh, a few years,' Cedric said carelessly. 'Long enough to have forgotten exactly when I came,' he added with a smile.

'I know the feeling. Even after three years I'm beginning to feel that way myself.'

Small-talk. Waste-of-time talk. Time he didn't have to spare, but Cedric was puzzling him. He never had in the past, but he was now.

'How long is Caitlin away for?'

'A few days, until she gets bored and comes home. Or, more likely, until she gets tired of her sister. Or falls out with her.'

'Where does she live?'

'The sister? Manchester way. On the outskirts.'

'I don't recall her ever mentioning her sister.'

'No, they're not that close. But occasionally contact is made.'

Jake nodded. He wasn't comfortable with the conversation. Cedric wasn't either, he sensed. Perhaps because he was still feeling guilty about his outburst last time they'd met.

'Is Caitlin well, Cedric?'

Cedric shrugged. 'You're never entirely well when you get to our age, Jake. But I know what you mean. Yes, she's well enough, thank you.'

'That's not why she's away?'

'No. Of course not.'

Cedric studied his coffee for a moment and glanced at his watch. He still seemed uncomfortable.

Jake wondered if he was being told the truth.

Then Cedric smiled and stirred himself. 'You can stay here, Jake. Plenty of room – even more than usual. And you'll be safe enough. Besides, it's a lot nicer than that God-awful pub!'

Jake laughed. 'The King's Arms isn't so bad. But I might take you up on that offer.'

'You're most welcome. And Tom won't mind if you move out. Nothing much bothers him. Just tell him you're going back to the cottage.'

Jake nodded. Maybe. He'd see. Something wasn't right, though.

He waited a moment and then said, 'I didn't know you read Arabic?'

Cedric glanced around at his bookshelves and smiled again. 'Not very well, but it is an old interest of mine.'

'You were out there?'

Jake waited, poised. The question suddenly seemed important. He wasn't quite sure why, but it did.

Cedric glanced at his watch and then nodded. 'Like you, Jake. The same firm. A bit earlier, of course, but the same firm.'

That was another surprise, though not as big a one as it would have been half-an-hour earlier.

'And Caitlin?'

'Her, too.'

Astonishing. That was all Jake could think. Absolutely bloody astonishing!

'You . . . what? Retired here?'

'We did. It was somewhere neither of us had any previous connection with.'

Anonymity, then, just as he himself had sought.

Jake took a deep breath. 'Did you know about me, Cedric?'

'Not at first.'

'But. . . .'

'I was informed, of course.'

Jake was stunned.

'They do keep track of us,' Cedric said gently. 'Surely you knew that?'

Jake shook his head. He wondered what else he didn't know, and who had told Cedric about him, and why.

He also wondered why Cedric kept looking at his watch, as if time was pressing. It was a gesture that made him uneasy.

'What about Sanderson? Did you know about him, as well?'

Cedric nodded. 'The Department set him up here. He wasn't well, poor chap. He'd had a bad time, and hadn't recovered as quickly as they'd hoped. They thought I might be able to help, if ever he needed support. Which he did, of course. Poor chap.'

Jesus Christ! Jake thought despairingly. It was beginning to sound as if he'd found an old lags' home, not anonymity, when he came here. He even began to wonder if coming here really had been his own idea. It had seemed it at the time, but . . . He could no longer be sure.

He didn't think he wanted much more of Cedric's company either. Not tonight. He wanted to get away. He'd have to find somewhere else to hole up.

'Sanderson's dead now, Cedric. What happened?'

Cedric shook his head. 'An accident, I hear. Or suicide? It's very sad. Not totally unexpected, though, given his state of mind.'

He looked up and shrugged. Jake let it go.

'Who told you about me, Ced?'

Cedric peered at him over the top of his heavy glasses. He considered the question carefully before replying. 'Will Rogers,' he said eventually. 'You knew him, didn't you? In the old days?'

Jake stared and shook his head in disbelief.

'He's a big man now, Jake. None bigger, in fact. Not in the Service. That's what I hear.'

CHAPTER TWENTY-ONE

On the way back to The King's Arms to collect his things and try to square Tom over the busted bathroom door and all the upset, he cut through the Narrow Nick, a yard-wide alley between the chemist's shop and the florist's.

The path was maybe thirty yards long. It had a street lamp at one end which cast long shadows. Blank stone walls stood on either side – the gable ends of buildings – disappearing up into the blackness.

That was where they were waiting for him. He knew at once he should have anticipated it, but his mind had been on other things. Cedric, in particular, who had pressed him very hard to stay. Big mistake.

Halfway down the Narrow Nick he saw his own shadow interfered with by someone else's and heard a soft footfall behind him. Simultaneously an indistinct figure appeared at the far end, blocking the alley.

They weren't going to shoot, he thought instantly. They would have done it already if they were. It would make too much noise. They wanted to take him quietly. Knives, probably.

He kept going, striding forward confidently. Weighing risks and options. He had seconds, two or three maybe, to make up his mind.

He stopped abruptly. He turned and glanced back along the alley. The guy behind him also stopped. Soft, sodium light from the street lamp at the entrance to the Narrow Nick played over his shoulder. He stood there, an immense black sentinel, blocking the escape route to Town Foot.

Movement from the other direction now. He could hear the soft shuffle and thud of the guy approaching from the far end at a steady pace. Jake could tell this one was ready for anything. They were both up for it. It was their big chance. They'd got him boxed and they knew it.

No time to run through all the mistakes he'd made, like not carrying a weapon. No time at all. None.

Go!

He braced his left hand and foot against one wall and right hand and foot against the opposite wall and sprang upwards, chimneying his way rapidly up into the blackness.

He heard feet pounding along the alley and ignored them. He worked hard, putting himself fast beyond reach of grasping hands and up above the pool of light shed by the street lamp.

Something hard hit him on the knee. He winced and closed his eyes for a moment, but managed to keep moving. He struggled on. Whatever they had thrown clattered to the ground, a knife, probably, but not a throwing knife. It hadn't stuck.

He was fifteen or twenty feet up now. His arms were aching like hell. He felt ready to collapse and his thigh muscles were not much better. He also had a bad case of the shakes setting in.

He paused and leaned his head back for a moment to glance up. The blackness of the night sky seemed paler. He was high enough now to be well out of reach, unless they abandoned caution and started shooting. He gritted his teeth and got going again, heading for the roof.

Provided his arms didn't give out he might make it; they were like soft rubber: quivering and shaking, they had little strength left in them. He tried to conserve it by transferring even more pressure to his legs, but the strength was ebbing out of them, too, and fast. They were shaking badly as well. Much more of this and they would lose their purchase, and he would drop.

He clamped his jaws together, closed his eyes and forced himself on, clawing his way up the walls. He had no choice. If he fell from this height it would be over anyway, whatever they had in mind down below.

Men's voices, loud and clear, broke the quiet. They were shouting and singing football chants. He paused, opened his eyes and glanced down. A group of men, fresh from the late delights of the King's Arms, or somewhere further afield, was entering the Narrow Nick. Five or six of them. He watched as they passed under the street lamp, and listened as they made their way along the alley. Their raucous voices reverberating to fill the confined space with argument and joyous celebration, sweeping all before them. Somebody had won.

He gave silent thanks for the disturbance and steeled himself to press on. He was just about done now – arms and legs both were numb and feeble. Pain soaked through his body. He was ready to drop. Only his mind refused to give up. He gave another lurch and inched upwards.

The brightness of the starry night sky gave him hope now. It loomed over a dark diagonal line that had to be the edge of the roof on one side of the alley. On the other, higher side there was still only a black, dark wall. He remembered then. There were more storeys above the chemist's than the flower shop: the wall of the Narrow Nick was higher on one side than the other.

He closed his eyes again, concentrated and heaved himself upward. One foot slipped off the wall. A wave of panic washed over him. Sudden doubt flooded his mind. He wouldn't make it. He was going to fall.

Not yet! he insisted through clenched teeth, jamming the rebellious foot back hard against the wall. Stick, you bastard!

A change of surface. Fingers felt a hard, sharp, sloping edge. He opened his eyes and glanced round. He was there.

A slate snapped off in his hand. He grimaced and wriggled higher, until he could get a forearm and then an elbow on to the sloping roof. His right arm. He pressed down hard, taking most of his weight on that arm. Then he pushed hard against the opposite wall with his left foot, and at the same time rotated his body so that he could get his left arm on to the roof as well.

His feet and legs dropped and trailed in the void. It was desperate for a moment, but his arms and upper body were on the roof now, and he wriggled and scrabbled until a lot more of him was on the roof. And, finally, all of him was there.

Not exactly safe, though. It was a slate roof with a steep pitch. He could feel his entire body aching to slide down the slope, trip over the edge and crash into Town Foot, but for the moment he couldn't do much about it. His strength was spent. He lay spreadeagled on his front, only friction holding him in place.

His pulse gradually slowed. His breath came easier. He stopped panting. His arms and legs ceased to shake. Muscles relaxed, became numb. He lay still, eyes closed, his face pressed hard against the cold slate, and was thankful it was too early in the night for dew to have formed and coated the slates with slime.

His thought processes began to work again. The football supporters had moved on. He raised his head and listened. No singing now. Only night sounds. A breeze whispering intermittently in the trees on the green. Small things flying fast close to his head, skimming across the roof. Somewhere a door banged in the strengthening breeze. He even fancied he could hear the hum of conversation from The King's Arms.

He had to get on. He raised his head and looked along the length of the roof. It wasn't a simple, flat expanse of slate. There were protrusions, obstacles, here and there. Attics, he supposed, and dormers. There would also be changes of level between the hotch-potch collection of ancient buildings that comprised the street.

He decided his best course would be to make his way up to the ridge, and then move along it until he found an escape route. On the ridge, if he could get that far, there would at least be something to hold on to. He could even straddle it if all else failed.

The steep pitch of the roof made upward progress awkward and hazardous. He placed his faith in friction and got on with it, inching his way ever higher.

He made it. He sat astride the ridge tiles and paused to take stock. He wondered where the two men from the alley had gone. Then he grimaced. He could guess exactly where they would have gone, and what they would be planning to do. They were busy trying to close loopholes and leaks. And removing obstacles. He was only one of them.

He pulled out his mobile and speed-dialled Dixie.

'Anna,' he said without preamble. 'Get her out. Now!'

CHAPTER TWENTY-TWO

She preferred the guest house to the pub. For one thing, it didn't smell musty; for another, it was quieter. There wasn't the background drone of voices, interspersed with bouts of manic laughter and breaking glass. Nor the creaking stairs and corridors that so characterized The King's Arms. She welcomed the quiet, and the calm. She needed to think.

Friday should be all right. It was such a simple, modest, low-key event that it couldn't fail to be, could it? Surely Jake's concerns were exaggerated? That would be why Ed didn't want her to bother with them. It sort of made sense now.

On the other hand . . . The attacks on Jake and poor Sanderson had actually happened, and they might be connected. Mightn't they? So why was Ed so adamant that she should ignore them?

She sighed and stretched. It was so quiet here, so peaceful, and she was very tired. Perhaps she would sleep tonight. It would make a welcome change if she did.

In the King's Arms she would never have heard them coming. Even if she had, she would have thought nothing of it. Just people. People passing by.

But it was different here. Nobody was just passing by.

And anyway they weren't. Passing by, that is. They were stood outside her door, trying to be quiet. Jake again? Somehow she didn't think so. Not now the ice between them was broken.

She took out her gun and checked it with her fingers in the darkness. She took off the safety catch. As the door handle squeaked and began to turn she got up from the bed and moved up beside the door.

She heard the lock click but a bolt stopped the door opening. She wondered what would happen next, and held her breath, finger already taking up pressure on the trigger.

Then they knocked on the door. Surprise gone, they might as well.

'Who is it?' she called, switching on the overhead light.

'Message from Section Six,' a low voice said. 'For you, Anna.'

Her section. She began to relax. Ed Donaldson must have changed his mind about something.

'One moment!'

She thought fast. It was unusual, communicating this way, sending someone instead of phoning, but reasonable. Ed could have other people here, as well as her. Possibly a lot of people, given the heightened security everywhere these days.

He could still have phoned her, but there were times when you didn't want to risk your message not getting through or being intercepted. Or it was complicated. Times when the direct route was best, if not the easiest.

She shrugged. Caution was all very well but you could think and worry yourself to death while you were being cautious.

She stepped across to the door and slid the bolt aside. The door opened. They came in quickly. Two of them. Both medium-height and slim. Not young, but tough-looking. She didn't know either of them.

One stepped round her and made his way to the window. She heard him making sure the curtains were fully closed.

The other, unsmiling, held out his hand. 'The gun, please. You're being relieved.'

'Relieved? What do you mean? What for?'

'The gun – now!'

The gun stayed where it was, held in front of her, pointing forward, but she realized she'd made a big mistake. She'd let them in.

'Show me some ID,' she snapped.

'The message,' he responded, still unsmiling, 'is that you're relieved of duty, and you're to come with us.'

'Show me some ID.'

He just stared at her.

'You!' she called, with a sideways glance at the one near the window. 'Come where I can see you.'

He didn't move.

'Don't be silly, Anna,' the first one said quietly. 'Give me the gun.'

The gun was holding him. But for how long? And she couldn't cover them both. Stalemate for the moment, but not for long probably.

'I'm making a phone call,' she said, wanting to hear Ed tell her it was true.

'Ed Donaldson sent us,' the man in front of her said, as if reading her mind.

So he knew both their names, she thought despondently. It must be all right. Legitimate, anyway. Not right, though. No way was it right! Pulling her out like this? And for what? For no reason, no good reason.

Well, she wasn't having it! Not without hearing it from Ed himself.

'I'm calling him,' she said, turning towards the table where she'd put her bag and her phone. 'I'm not taking the word of someone I don't know, and who won't show me any ID.'

They let her reach the table and pick up the phone. Very clever. As she jiggled gun and phone, they moved in unison. They were good, too, well practised. They made her feel like the beginner she was.

The one near the window wrapped his arms around her from behind and squeezed hard, pinioning everything. The breath left her body with a whoosh. She tried to rake his shin with her heel but she missed, and in any case she wasn't wearing shoes.

The other one stepped forward and simply took gun and phone from her hands. She spat at him. He straightened up, glaring and hit her hard in the face with the back of his hand.

'Don't ever do that again,' he warned, wiping away the spittle.

'Who the hell do you think—'

'Shut up!' he snapped. 'You should have listened, you stupid bitch. You were told what to do, and what not to do, but you ignored that advice. Now you'd better start listening.

'You're coming with us. We can do it the easy way. But if you want to do it the hard way, we can cope.'

She stared at him for a moment. Then she nodded. 'Wait till I see Ed

Donaldson,' she said bitterly, beginning to wonder now if she ever would.

They stretched tape across her mouth and snapped plasti-cuffs on her wrists. Then a black hood over her head. She tried to hold back the panic by rehearsing in her mind the formal complaint she would make, if she ever got the chance. But the strongest language she could come up with didn't seem to match the occasion.

CHAPTER TWENTY-THREE

So they were taking her. Not just talking to her. Dixie had wondered if that would happen. It meant they were serious.

She waited. She waited for the two men to separate. One came out of the building and strode quickly round the corner towards the parked car.

She'd seen enough. She jumped off the parapet and abseiled down the front of the guest house. When she reached the pavement she pulled the thin rope down after her and stuffed it into the daypack she carried. Then she stepped into the shadow of an adjacent doorway.

The car arrived on sidelights only, engine quietly humming. As the driver was getting out, Dixie stepped close and jammed her gun into his ear. He froze, one foot on the pavement, the other still inside the car. One hand holding on to the door handle, the other gripping the steering wheel.

'Be still!' she snapped.

He didn't move.

Working quickly, she showed she could do things by the book as well as they could. She plasti-cuffed one hand to the steering wheel and the other to a grab handle set above the door. Then she pulled a black hood over his head.

'See how you like it!' she snapped grimly.

'You're making a big mistake.'

'Yeah? We'll see about that.'

Then she pulled up the hood and stuck a strip of tape across his mouth to complete the job, the same as they'd done to Anna.

'You're lucky I don't just shoot you now, you sonovabitch!' she told him, 'and get it over with.'

She turned away then and stepped back into the doorway to wait. She didn't have to wait long. Seconds only. She heard the front door of the guest house open. Shadows appeared on the pavement. She moved fast.

He was good. He sensed her. Even before he saw his partner's predicament, he sensed Dixie coming and swung round, gun arm rising.

Dixie fired first. Two sharp cracks – body shots that crumpled him in a heap. She kicked the gun out of his hand as he went down. Then she crouched and checked for a pulse in his neck. He muttered a few words that surprised her. Then he stopped. Immediate danger over. He wouldn't be getting up again.

She looked round. Anna was frozen to the spot.

'It's OK.,' Dixie said, getting back to her feet. 'Don't worry, Anna. The cavalry's here.'

She reached up and pulled the hood off Anna's head. Then she brought out a serious knife and cut through the plastic tie on Anna's wrists with a deft stroke.

She began to ease the tape from Anna's mouth, but thought better of it. 'You do it,' she said, letting go and stepping back.

It was too dark to read the other woman's expression but Dixie sensed she was in shock. 'It's OK., Anna,' she said again. 'I'm a friend. Come on now. Quick! Let's go.'

She grabbed her by the arm and began to hustle her away.

'Who the hell are you?' Anna asked belligerently when they were round the corner and heading through the churchyard. She was recovering fast.

'It's a long story,' Dixie said, quickening her pace. 'But I'm one of the good guys. I'm an old friend of Jake's.'

'Jake? Jake Ord? How . . . No, stop! Just stop.'

She slowed. Dixie grabbed her arm. 'We can't stop. Not yet, Anna. We need to get out of here.'

'And I need to know what's going on,' Anna said firmly. She pulled away from Dixie and stood facing her.

They stood still on the stone-flagged path between the yew trees and the ancient, weathered sandstone gravestones, and they stared at one another.

'We've got to go,' Dixie said.

Anna spoke carefully, slowly. 'You're not one of Ed's team, are you? You're not from the Service?'

Dixie grimaced and cast keen eyes all around, working the shadows. Then she sighed. 'We don't have a lot of time, Anna,' she said gently.

'I need to know what's going on.'

Dixie nodded. 'Do you trust Jake?'

'Trust Jake? I hardly know him.'

'But do you trust him?'

'As much as I would any man I've had a half-hour conversation with.'

Dixie smiled reluctantly and nodded. 'I've got a decision to take very soon,' she said. 'We can do this conversation somewhere safe – relatively safe. Or I'm going to have to leave you to cope on your own. I can't afford to hang around. It's too dangerous.'

Anna hesitated. This strange woman had got her out of a hole, but that wasn't enough. 'I'm going to call my boss,' she said, reaching automatically for her mobile, forgetting a lot of what had just happened, forgetting she didn't even have a mobile. Much in the way of clothes either, for that matter.

'No!' Dixie snapped. 'No calls – to anyone.'

'It's my boss. He'll be wondering. . . .'

'Later. Are you coming with me or not?'

Another moment. Then Anna nodded reluctantly. She hadn't got her mobile anyway.

'OK. Let's go.'

'Where to?'

'Not far.'

Dixie led the way along the riverside and then back into the west end of the village. She stopped beside the salmon ladder at the weir and brought out her own mobile.

'I've got her,' she said quickly into it. 'You off the roof yet?'

Anna strained to hear but only heard one half of the conversation.

'Ten minutes,' Dixie said, ending the call.

'Ten minutes?' Anna repeated.

'We're rendezvousing with Jake.'

Anna nodded and wondered if Jake would know what was going on any more now than he had the last time she'd spoken to him.

She also wondered about this strange woman beside her. She wondered about her a lot.

The strange woman shepherded Anna to a car parked nearby, in a little clearing where there was a pile of gravel and salt for use on winter roads. She used a remote to unlock the car. In the light from the interior Anna got her first good look at the woman's face and realized that she wasn't as young as she'd assumed. It was a good face though, she decided, one she felt instinctively she could trust.

Dixie noticed her looking. 'What?' she said.

Anna shrugged. She was reluctant to ask the woman again who she was. It made her seem the amateur she felt and knew herself to be.

They stood on opposite sides of the car, the doors open, staring at each other.

'Get in!' Dixie said.

'Where are we going?'

'I told you. To meet Jake.'

'Where, though?'

'His place.'

'The cottage?'

The woman nodded and got into the car. 'I'm Dixie,' she said, settling herself behind the steering wheel.

Anna got into the passenger seat and slammed the door shut after her. 'You seem to know my name,' she pointed out.

'Jake told me.' Dixie started the engine. 'Ten minutes,' she said. 'Be patient.'

That put an end to the conversation, such as it was. Anna sat back and waited. Ten minutes was nothing. She could do that. She could wait that long, but no longer.

Dixie edged on to the road and drove cautiously into the west end of the village. She turned into the back lane that led to the track running out to Jake's cottage. She drove at first on side lights only, switching to headlights when they were a little way along the track.

'Is it safe?' Anna asked.

'Maybe.' Dixie glanced sideways at her and added in a softer tone, 'It should be – for the moment.'

Right now, Anna didn't really care whether it was safe or not. Or about anything else either. A reaction to what had happened was setting in. She didn't feel good and she was cold. She was shivering. She just wanted some peace and quiet. And heat.

'You OK.?' Dixie asked,

Anna nodded. 'I will be,' she said, trying to sound tougher than she felt. 'I'm just a bit cold. Was he dead, that man?'

Dixie nodded. Then she said, 'You're not a field agent, are you?'

'No.' Anna shook her head, glad to have that out of the way. 'I do research. This is my first field assignment.'

'Hang in there! You're doing OK.'

Anna was surprised how sympathetic the other woman sounded. 'I'm OK.,' she said with new-found determination.

'Sure you are.'

Dixie slowed right down and changed into second to negotiate a place where storm water had hollowed out the track. 'If it's any consolation for what happened back there,' she said, 'the same would have happened to you if I hadn't been around. Those guys were real mean, and they meant business.'

Anna shivered. She believed it. But what was their business?

'Are you American?' she asked.

Dixie didn't reply.

CHAPTER TWENTY-FOUR

They arrived. The cottage was in darkness. Dixie parked next to a stone wall alongside the cottage. She spoke a couple of words into her mobile, which was still switched on, and got the answer she wanted. She switched off the engine.

'Let's go!' she said, opening her door.

Anna followed reluctantly.

Jake appeared out of the darkness and led the way through the yard and into the cottage.

'How are you, Anna?' he asked as soon as they were inside, in the dim light from an oil lamp turned low.

'OK.'

She didn't look OK, but he let it go. Nobody looked their best shivering in their nightware, which in Anna's case was the white T-shirt he'd seen once before.

He pulled a fleece jacket from a peg near the door and slipped it over her shoulders. She took it without comment and pulled it close around her.

'We'll find you some other stuff in a minute,' he said.

Then he took them both into the kitchen, where he'd pinned a heavy, dark-coloured tablecloth over the plastic-sheathed window. Another oil lamp gave a soft glow to the room.

'The best I could do,' he said, seeing Dixie eyeing the window.

'You've lost none of your old skills, I see.' She grinned and said, 'Is that coffee I can smell in that there pot?'

'Americans!' he said, shaking his head and giving Anna a what-can-you-do look.

Anna stared back at him, blank-faced.

'Sit down – please!' he urged, pulling a couple of chairs out from beneath the table.

Dixie needed no second invitation. Anna followed slowly, almost reluctantly, as if still dazed.

Jake lifted the coffee pot off the wood-burning stove. 'So what's been going on?' he asked, bringing three mugs and the coffee pot to the table.

The bald facts didn't take long to recite. Dixie went first. Then Jake asked questions and said his piece. Afterwards he glanced at Anna, who had remained silent throughout.

'Don't ask me,' she said, her voice unexpectedly shrill. 'I've no fucking idea what's going on! Except there's a man dead back there. Shot by . . . by your friend, here.'

It was said with spirit, Jake noted with relief. A bit hysterical maybe, but at least they didn't have a basket case on their hands.

'Well,' he said diplomatically, 'none of us really knows what's going on. Yet.'

'Me least of all,' Anna said bitterly. 'And it's my fucking assignment! Or it was.'

She looked from one to the other of them and added, 'Are we safe here?'

Dixie stirred her coffee and gazed speculatively at the ruined window.

'For the moment,' Jake said. 'They don't know where we are. Whoever they are. Besides, we've hit them pretty hard, and they can't have unlimited manpower.'

'Two men down,' Dixie contributed in an equally calm tone. 'But they have at least another two or three in the village, plus whoever is running this thing.'

'And that's another question,' Jake pointed out. 'Just who is running it?'

'I need to call my boss,' Anna said with a start, as if suddenly remembering why she was in Cragley in the first place.

'Not a good idea,' Jake said. 'At the moment.'

'Why not?' she said belligerently. 'I'm sick of people telling me what I can and can't do!'

'What would you tell him? What would you tell him that he doesn't know already?'

She stared at him until she took in his meaning. 'You're not suggesting. . . ?'

Jake shrugged and reached for the coffee pot. 'Think about it,' he suggested, still calm, as he poured them all a refill.

'I don't understand.'

'It's not easy, but . . .' He shrugged and paused. 'Who instructed you to stay away from me? Who told you I was talking rubbish and making it up about the attacks on me?'

Anna said nothing.

'How did the guys that came for you know your name?' Jake continued in an inexorably reasonable way. 'And how is it they were able to remind you you'd been warned already? And why were they so brutal, unless they were worried you might talk to someone, and had been given instructions to avert that at all costs?'

'Stop it!' she snapped, glowering fiercely at him. 'Stop it now. This is preposterous.'

Jake shrugged. He could see she would have to come to terms with it in her own way, and in her own time.

'Who is your boss?' Dixie asked.

'I'm not getting into that.'

Dixie nodded and looked thoughtfully at Jake.

'Let's recount?' he suggested. He picked up his mug and took a sip of coffee. 'Let's see if we can make sense of this.'

Anna looked ready for a moment to argue. Then she changed her mind and shut up.

Again Jake ran through what had been happening in the past few days. 'Finally, Anna,' he concluded, 'someone – your boss, we believe – wants you out of the way. Presumably because he failed to stop you talking to the wrong sort of people, and asking awkward questions.'

He stopped to draw breath, and to let Anna think about it and join up the dots. There was a lot to take in. He hoped he'd covered all the angles.

'Another question,' Dixie said quietly, breaking the long silence, 'is whether there really are two outfits in the field, locked in combat, or. . . .'

'Or?' Jake prompted, realizing where she was going, but wanting to hear her say it anyway.

'Or just the one.'

They were quiet again after that, all three of them trying to get their heads round the questions raised, and the implications.

If they ruled out good guys versus bad guys, Jake reflected, that meant some of the same people who were supposedly providing background security were actually planning to assassinate the visiting Royal, as well as himself and Sanderson. Nightmare!

'It's nonsense,' Anna said eventually, quietly but somehow without conviction. 'The Security Service planning a Royal assassination – and the rest of it? Nonsense!'

'Isn't it?' Jake said. 'Absolute nonsense.' He waited a moment and then said, 'So who's your boss?'

She gazed at him. He could see the muscles in her face working overtime beneath the smooth, pale skin. In the soft lamplight his heart went out to her. Her big chance to jump-start her career in the field, and it had come to this. Complications and dangers that could never have occurred to her, and now possible conspiracy and betrayal, as well.

'Ed Donaldson.'

He was disappointed. The name meant nothing to him. But how could it? He and Sanderson had been MI6, which surely would have no locus here. Anna was almost certainly either MI5 or the Met. He still didn't know which.

He looked at Dixie and shook his head. She shrugged.

'It's not your fault,' he said, turning back to Anna.

'Of course it bloody isn't!'

'You've done nothing wrong, Anna. Don't worry about it.'

She tossed her head impatiently.

Dixie said, 'What do you think, Jake? Cancel the Royal visit?'

'We're not in any position to do that. We. . . .'

He stopped, seeing her grinning at him.

He shook his head and gave her a reluctant smile. 'All right, all right! You're only kidding. No-one would listen to us anyway. A Yank and a has-been?'

'Well, what are we going to do?' Anna asked. 'Maybe I should just go home, and report into the office tomorrow. Hand in my resignation.'

'No, don't do that,' Dixie said, shaking her head. 'That would be a mistake, and it wouldn't get you off the hook anyway.'

Jake gazed at her thoughtfully. Dixie was right. If Anna was a threat here, she wouldn't cease to be a threat back in London. He wouldn't care to put money on her lasting very long there, or anywhere else now. The stakes were too high.

But there were options.

He looked across at Dixie. 'Are you thinking what I'm thinking?' he asked.

'Probably.' She gave him a big sunny smile and added, 'I haven't come all this way for nothing, Jake. I want a result.'

'You and me both.'

He got up and began to wander around the kitchen, wondering if they could do it. He was sure about Dixie and himself. They'd done plenty before, in the not so distant past. And, surprisingly perhaps, he still seemed to be up for it. The adrenaline was flowing. In fact, in a perverse sort of way, he was almost enjoying it. Like old times!

But Anna?

He didn't want her getting hurt any more than she had been already. They couldn't exclude her, though. They owed her and she was seriously at risk now, thanks to him.

There was also the fact that he was drawn to her. He liked her – a lot. He didn't want anything to happen to her and he didn't want to disappoint her. So he had to give her the choice of remaining part of it or not.

'We can't stop HRH's visit,' he reiterated, as if thinking aloud. 'If we try, they'll laugh at us or lock us up. Maybe both, maybe worse.

'On the other hand, it's going to be difficult to block any assassination plan. We're not really sure who's involved, for a start. Only that they're serious, and dangerous, and possibly some sort of renegade security group.

'Our strong card is that we know they won't ignore us. They want us out of the game and off the board, preferably before the main action starts. We can use that knowledge. It gives us an edge.'

He paused there. Dixie would know where he was heading. He wanted to see if Anna did, too.

'You think they'll try again?' Anna asked.

'I'm sure of it.'

'So how do we deal with it? What do we do?'

He breathed a sigh of relief. She was coming round. She was climbing on board.

'Nothing,' he said. 'At least, Dixie goes back out into the wild, to run interference – as I believe you would call it?' he added with an innocent glance sideways.

Dixie smiled.

'And I stay here – and wait.'

'Wait for them to come?' Anna asked.

He nodded.

She thought it over and said, 'What about me? What do I do?'

'Well, you could return to London, as you suggested yourself, and take your chances. You could go back where you belong.'

'Or?'

'Or you could stay here.'

'With you?'

'With us.'

'Would I be any use to you?'

'You would be putting yourself in harm's way,' he said gently. 'Possibly even more here than in London.'

'But would I be any use?'

'I'm sure you would.'

'I need to think about it.'

'Take your time.'

'I've thought about it.'

'And?'

'I like how you two do things,' she said with a reluctant grin. 'I'll stay.'

CHAPTER TWENTY-FIVE

'There's just one thing,' Anna said.

Jake looked at her.

'You don't have any proof a Royal assassination is planned, do you?'

He shook his head.

'Just that someone has killed Sanderson and tried to kill you?'

'That's right.'

She nodded and seemed satisfied. She'd got her point across. Made a contribution.

It was true, though, he thought. She was right. No proof at all. He hoped they were not building a house of cards with all this theorizing.

He glanced at Dixie. 'You tell her,' he suggested.

'Nothing much to tell.' Dixie stretched and flexed, and tossed her hair back. 'Like Jake admitted, we don't know it for a fact. We're theorizing, but it's what you have to do in the field. Build constructs, use your judgement and act. If you wait till a Commission of Enquiry explores the options and reports with all the evidence and analyses, everyone who matters could be dead. This way, if we're wrong, we're just wrong. If we're right, someone important might live. And so might we,' she added with a dry chuckle.

Jake took the first watch. Dixie and Anna found beds and were soon quiet, leaving him to prowl undisturbed.

The cottage was noisy at night, but he was familiar with the sounds it made as it cooled and settled. He welcomed them, the creaks and groans, the cracks and sighs. He would have missed them had they not been there. Equally, he would have noticed instantly had one occurred that didn't belong.

For a while he sat in soft lamplight in the kitchen, watching the flame flicker just above the wick – listening – waiting. Then he blew out the flame and sat in darkness, restoring his night vision, considering and waiting.

Occasionally he got up and moved around the cottage, listening, trying to sense anything out of the ordinary.

He wondered what difference it would make if they did manage to take him out, as well as Sanderson. What would they be able to do then that they couldn't do now? He could think of nothing.

Something else worrying him was Cedric; he had become a different man. The new Cedric had difficulty with the truth. Or, at least, he wasn't always prepared to reveal it. There was no way, for instance, that Cedric could believe Sanderson's death had been an accident. Yet he'd wanted Jake to entertain the idea.

What it meant was that Cedric was not to be trusted. Jake knew he was going to have to get used to this new version of the man he'd thought of as a good friend.

And what about Caitlin? What chance was there she'd really gone to visit her sister? According to her, she didn't even have a sister! He could recall quite clearly a conversation in which she had said that she, just like him, had no siblings.

So it didn't add up. None of it did.

A whisper of movement brought him spinning round and down into a fighting crouch.

'It's time,' Dixie said quietly. 'Go get some rest, Jake.'

He hadn't heard her until it was too late – she was so good, but he could see her now. He turned back to the window and realized there was a hint of grey in the hitherto black sky. Morning was about to break.

'There's something strange going on with Cedric,' he said.

'Your friend with the antiques shop?'

He nodded.

Dixie waited.

'First, he told me to keep away. I was trouble.'

'Seems reasonable.'

'Yet they are my friends, the closest friends I have here. And at that point there wasn't any trouble, as far as he was supposed to know. I'd said nothing. I'd loaned them my cat and said I might be going away for a while, but that was all.'

'Could he have seen, or guessed, something?'

'I don't see how. He must have talked to someone.' Jake thought it over and shook his head. 'And now he wants to help.'

'What are friends for?'

'And – get this! – now he tells me he was in the service. He knew I was, and he knew Sanderson was, too. Also, he knows Will Rogers.'

He stopped there and watched Dixie's face.

'Wow!' she said after a moment.

He nodded. 'That's what I think, too.'

'So he's real.'

'He must be.'

'Is it just coincidence that you are all here, in this little village?'

'It doesn't look like it. At one time I might have thought so, but now . . .' He shrugged. 'Cedric tells me Sanderson – Doug Kennedy to you and me in the old days – was in poor health, mentally even more than physically, I think. He was beached here, so Cedric could keep an eye on him.'

'Was Cedric here before you came?'

That was another question.

'I'd always assumed so. Now I'm beginning to wonder. He didn't answer directly when I asked him how long he'd been here.'

'It seems unlikely that all of you could have decided independently to live here in Cragley. You did, you say, but Sanderson didn't. And maybe Cedric didn't either.'

Jake stood up and moved to the window. Beyond the old outhouse he could see the dark slope of the hillside, and above that clear blue sky. There was no frost, not yet. He expected it soon though. He could have gone anywhere in the world but he'd come here, to north Northumberland, as if by instinct. Had it really been an independent decision? He wished he could be certain. Had he spoken to anyone? Been given advice? He couldn't remember.

And exactly how had Cedric ended up here?

'You say he's being helpful now?' Dixie said, pressing gently.

He nodded.

'What about his wife?'

'Caitlin? She's not here.'

'Why not?'

'She's gone to visit her sister near Manchester.'

'Cedric told you?'

He nodded.

'Do you believe him?'

He said nothing for a moment. He stared at the hillside some more. Then he turned and shrugged. 'At first I had no reason not to,' he said.

'And now?'

Now he didn't know. Why should Cedric have told him the truth about that, when there had been so many other lies and evasions and concealments?

'Where else would she be?' he asked uncertainly.

Dixie shrugged. 'All I know is that your friend doesn't always tell you the truth. He tells you what suits him.'

'True.' He took stock for a moment. 'Caitlin once told me she didn't have a sister or a brother.' He paused and added, 'She might have been lying, I suppose.'

Dixie said nothing. He guessed she was thinking they were his friends; he ought to know. But he didn't.

'Think you could find her?' he asked heavily.

'Depends how much time I have. I could try.'

'I think you should. We need to know if Cedric was lying about that, as well.'

She nodded. Then she smiled. 'Get some sleep now, Jake. You're going to need it.'

It was fully daylight when he awoke. He glanced at his watch and saw it was almost eight. He grimaced. He hadn't meant to sleep so long.

He pushed the covers back and rolled off the bed. After a pit-stop in the bathroom he made his way downstairs. Anna was sitting at the kitchen table. She looked up and smiled. That made him feel better. She seemed to like him again.

'All quiet?' he asked.

She nodded. 'Dixie left. She didn't say where she was going.'

'She doesn't like to be cooped up indoors.'

'I was going to wake you in a little while, Jake, but you needed some sleep.'

'Thanks. I'm fine now. How about you?'

She shrugged. She stared at him and pulled a face. 'I can't believe what happened last night.'

'It could have been worse.'

'Probably. But it could have been better, too. Jake, what's happening here?'

He shook his head. He'd already given her all the answers he had.

'I know, I know!' she said. 'Silly me, expecting all to be revealed in the full light of day. It's not like that, is it?'

'Not in your line of work,' he said pointedly. 'The fog of war is an appropriate phrase that comes to mind. It's an old one, but it is still apt.'

'My line of work?' she murmured. She shook her head, as if mystified to be in this position. 'I wonder what Ed's up to. It's a pity he didn't take me into his confidence.'

'We're past that point, Anna,' he said gently. 'Remember? Ed seems to be a large part of the problem.'

'Oh, I don't think so! Do you, really?'

'I do. We went all through that last night.'

'Yes, but. . . .'

He didn't say anything more. She needed to get used to the idea. No need to pile on the pressure.

But from what Dixie had told him, and from his own experience and instinct, the men who had come for Anna last night had been serious. She might have survived another hour or two, but not much more. She knew too much – even if she didn't know it all.

'The phone line's dead,' she said now.

He looked at her and raised an eyebrow.

'It went dead a couple of hours ago. They must have cut it.'

So something was happening.

'They're coming for us, aren't they?'

He nodded. 'Probably.'

He eyed her closely, wondering if she would hold up.

'I'm OK,' she said softly with a smile.

He smiled back. She actually looked OK now. She was getting used to this new world she had entered.

'And another thing...' she added. 'There's no coverage for your mobile. I can't raise a signal with it.'

He grinned. 'Not all servers reach out here.'

'So we're cut off?'

He didn't bother replying. Time she used her brain. She'd heard him and Dixie talking.

'How long have we got before they come?'

'I don't know. The normal pattern is for these things to kick-off just before dawn.' He shrugged and added, 'Maybe they couldn't get organized in time.'

'Well, it will have to be soon,' she said. 'They're running out of time.'

He nodded agreement.

She was right. It was Tuesday today. The Royal visit was scheduled for Friday. The next couple of days were going to be long ones.

'We should eat,' he said.

'I'm not hungry.'

'Eat anyway. Eggs OK?'

She nodded and sighed. 'You're right. Food is fuel?'

'And it's energy. We're going to need that.'

He moved to the fridge and began to take things out.

'I found some trousers and socks,' she said. 'Hope you don't mind?'

'I wondered why I couldn't see your legs any more.'

She gave him the lop-sided smile he was getting used to, as he turned back to his task. He refrained from saying he preferred how she'd looked before.

'And Dixie gave me her spare gun,' she said quietly.

He glanced round again and saw her turning a pistol over in her hands. 'You OK with that?'

'I think so.' She stood up and gave him a smile. 'I'll do the rounds while you're making breakfast.'

'OK.'

He felt relief. She'd recovered.

CHAPTER TWENTY-SIX

'Who was the woman?'

'I don't know, Boss.'

'But you saw her?'

'Not really. It happened too fast.'

Sweet Jesus! Happened too fast!

'Tell me what you did see.'

'Not much. It was dark. She stuck a gun in my ear and said don't fucking move.'

'So you didn't move?'

The other man shook his head.

'But you are sure it was a woman?'

'Yeah. I heard her speak.'

He closed his eyes for a moment and let the fury wash over him silently. Fucking Grey!

He shook his head, more in sorrow than anger. How on earth had Williams put up with him?

'So what did you hear her say? What did she sound like?'

'United States.'

'She sounded like . . .' He paused and stopped himself. Some of them were better with the language than others. 'You mean she was American?'

'Yeah. Think so.'

What did that mean? He couldn't imagine. Or, rather, he didn't want to imagine. He wanted to stick with the facts. They were complicated enough.

'And she shot Williams?'

'Yeah. In cold blood. He done nothing!'

That seemed unlikely.

'Did you see what happened?'

A reluctant negative followed. 'Was strapped up, Boss.'

Yeah, yeah. And had a gun in your ear.

'How many shots did she fire?'

'Two, maybe three.'

'Try again.'

'Two. I'm pretty sure two.'

'Did Williams fire any?'

'Nah! Didn't have a chance, poor bastard.'

'Did he have his weapon out?'

'Yeah. Sure. To take the other woman – that fucking Anna!'

He thought quickly. He visualised it, the way he'd been told. Williams had been good. In every way. Smart, aggressive, resourceful. Good with weapons. So the woman had been better. That was the only logical conclusion.

Who the hell was she? And why was she watching, protecting, the Mason woman?

For a moment he wondered if colleagues from another service could have been keeping an eye on things. Then he ruled that out. It wasn't possible.

It wasn't possible that the CIA was either. Just not possible.

It had happened, though. He couldn't deny it, but for now that option would just have to be filed in the pending tray. He couldn't afford to let it clutter up the works. The timetable was tight enough already.

Pity about Williams. He was a good man. He'd have to go easy on Grey, as well. The two of them had worked well together. Better get him out of the way.

'Boss?'

'Yes?'

'The woman. She called me a sonovabitch!'

He smiled at last. Grey's outrage was palpable.

'Don't worry about it. Go back to the house, and wait. Take it easy.'

'The fucking farm?'

'The fucking farm,' he agreed with a wince. They all watched far too many American movies.

If she'd called him that, she certainly was American. He wondered again who she was. He could have done without the uncertainty.

CHAPTER TWENTY-SEVEN

She was different now, less assured, more cautious. And she was definitely less amused by the world. He couldn't blame her.

'How long have you been with the Department?'

'A couple of years.'

'Like it?'

'Yes. Well . . . I did until yesterday.'

Now she wasn't sure. It was serious now. Her own life in the balance, as well as the lives of other people. It made a difference. Join the club! he thought.

'You did well,' she said suddenly. 'So did Dixie. All that,' she added, shaking her head. 'So unexpected.'

'It always is unexpected. You're always on the back foot in this game. You just have to respond to what gets thrown at you.'

'They've just used me,' she said bitterly.

He turned away, keeping his distance and waiting to see which way she would go. He didn't want her to collapse in a heap but if she was going to do that, it would be better to do it now while things were quiet.

'What are we going to do?' she asked in the quiet stillness.

'We?' he asked sharply, turning back to her.

'We.' She nodded and added, 'We're in it together now, remember?'

'That's right. We are,' he said with relief. 'Well, we're going to give them a hammering. We're going to win.'

He knew they couldn't do it on their own, though. They couldn't do everything. Especially now the police seemed to have him fingered as a

villain. Anna, as well, probably. Something was amiss at Five and Six, if
not the Met.

So if that was the case, who did it leave? The locals? He smiled grimly
as he thought of Sergeant Will Taylor, the self-confessed thirty-year man.
Solid as a rock but. . . .

'What are you smiling about?'

He glanced sideways at her and laughed. 'Smiling? Me?'

'You're always doing it.' she said tartly. 'I can't imagine what you can
be so happy about.'

Happy? Him? Now?

Yet, in a strange way, maybe he was. Not happy, as such, perhaps, but
… well, happier. Why not admit it? Feeling good, at least. Better. Doing
something he once was good at, something he hadn't done for a long
time but had found he could still handle.

'I was just thinking the Met boys are not up to much. Foolishly, I'd
assumed they would welcome my assistance – not want to lock me up.'

'You're being naïve, Jake.'

She smiled as she said it. He smiled back.

'What about the locals?' she said.

'What about them?'

'It's their patch. Why not talk to them?'

'The village sergeant? Will Taylor?'

'It doesn't have to be him, does it? Someone at Force HQ, I was thinking. Someone in Special Branch. The sergeant should be able to give you
a name.'

'Think it would make a difference?'

She gave him a big grin. 'Just try it, Jake. Try it and see.'

He shook his head and said in sorrow, 'You're wasted on them, Anna.
Do you know that?'

She nodded and grinned again.

Damn! he thought. He did like her.

'Will? It's Jake Ord.'

'Where are you, Jake?'

The voice was suspicious. He knew something.

'Will, I. . . .'

'Come into the station, lad. I'm just about to go there myself.'

Coming up to eleven, and the one hour of each day someone was in attendance at the village police station. There would be lost dogs; found dogs; car damaged overnight; a rubbish bin turned upside-down: the usual crime wave. A Royal assassination would make a change.

'I want to get in touch with someone in Special Branch, in Ponteland.'

'Who?'

'I don't know. That's why I'm ringing you. I need a name. Someone good. Someone I can talk to in confidence.'

'Come and see me, Jake. I'm just about to leave the house. I'll be there in five minutes. We can talk about it then.'

'Can't do that, Will. I think you know why, but I need a name urgently. It's important.'

During the silence that followed he could visualize the expression on Will's face. He was risking a lot. His pension most of all. To a thirty-year man, that would be what mattered most now. For that reason, Jake said nothing about his troubles. He wouldn't compromise the future of the man who looked after Cragley.

'Bob Cunningham,' Will said quietly. 'I can give you his direct number. He's a good man.'

Jake wrote name and phone number down on a pad.

'Thanks, Will.'

'Look after yourself, bonnie lad. Take care.'

'I'll do my best. Thanks again, Will. I'll buy you a pint in the King's Arms when I see you next.'

'I'm supposed to be cutting down. Doctor's orders.'

'*One*, I said!'

He rang off, Will's hearty laughter still booming in his ears. Anna raised an eyebrow.

'So far, so good,' he told her.

Then he frowned thoughtfully and added, 'There's something else I'd like to do now. Can you manage on your own for an hour or two?'

'No, not for one moment!' she said, glaring. Then she smiled. 'What is it?' she asked.

'I need to go into the village to check something out.'

'How are you going to do that?'

'I'll go over the moor on foot.'

'Bring me back some chocolate. I can't find any anywhere in this house.'

He waited until Cedric had left the house. Then he went round the back and managed to open a small upper window in an outhouse. He put his arm through the gap and tried to reach the catch on the big window below. He couldn't quite do it, but with the aid of a loop of string he found in a dustbin he managed. He sighed with relief and climbed through the gap.

He found himself in the back kitchen, the place where much of Cedric's pot making went on. There was dust everywhere. He was clearly a messy worker, Cedric. As he stepped across the floor, he scuffed the dust behind him, to avoid leaving footprints. When he reached the door-way, he picked up a cloth and wiped the soles of his shoes. Then he stepped into the hall and paused to think.

Something was going on with Cedric. He didn't know what. Had no idea what he was looking for, but Cedric's house seemed a good place to start.

A rapid tour of the house revealed nothing out of the ordinary. Nothing to attract suspicion or concern. There were no locked rooms and nothing was hidden. Everything was as it should be. It was a dark, gloomy house with small windows, typical of the style popular at the time it was built, and it kept out all but the necessary minimum of light. And there were plenty of creaking stairs.

A sudden noise had him wheeling round. Apache! He spoke to the cat as it came to him, rubbing itself against his leg. He bent down to stroke him and tickle his ears.

'I haven't abandoned you,' he said gravely. 'Think of it as a holiday, a change of scene. We'll be back together again soon enough – if you'll still have me!'

Satisfied, the cat left him, reassured, perhaps. Or else he could hear mice beginning to play, down in the cellar.

In Cedric's study, he made for the phone. It was a complicated looking affair, the base unit for several phones kept around the house. Working quickly, he checked the voicemail and the record of calls. Only one message. Everything else had been cleared. Either Cedric didn't get many calls or he made a practice of wiping everything clean a.s.a.p. It seemed surprising for a business, which was what The Gallery was supposed to be.

He re-played the remaining message. It was from Caitlin; he recognised her voice. A very simple message with no frills, it said nothing unnecessary.

'I am safe and well, Cedric.'

Just that.

He re-played it a couple of times. She was safe and well. What the hell did that mean? Nothing of the kind, obviously. The opposite, in fact.

He made a note of the number, a mobile number. Then he left.

'There was nothing else on the phone?'

Jake shook his head. 'Everything had been cleaned off. He probably does that automatically – good housekeeping.'

Dixie frowned. 'So that one message was very important to him. He kept it. Are you sure it was his wife?'

'It was Caitlin. No doubt about that.'

'Maybe he just wanted to hear her voice. Sentimental old man.'

Jake didn't think that was it. Not at all.

'Tell me again what she said.'

He repeated the phrase. It was an easy one to remember. And very ominous, the more so the more he thought about it.

Dixie sighed. 'You're probably right.'

'I think so. She's not visiting her sister at all. Somebody's got her somewhere.'

'So Cedric had to choose between you and his wife?'

'It looks like it.'

Cedric wouldn't have had much difficulty deciding who to choose. Jake couldn't blame him. It was disappointing, but entirely natural.

It was also understandable, which Cedric's behaviour had not been until now. In a way, that was a relief, too.

'You think the phone call was made from wherever they have her stashed?' Dixie asked.

'I have no idea, but it seems a reasonable bet.'

'I'll get on it right away.'

'Talk to Anna. See if she can access mobile phone records.'

'Oh, yeah! Good idea, boss.'

He glared at her.

She grinned back. 'Just being co-operative, boss.'

He shook his head and sighed. 'Just do it! Do it any way you can.'

CHAPTER TWENTY-EIGHT

'I'm scared,' she whispered with a shiver.

'That's all right,' he said. 'If you weren't scared, it could only be because you were stupid – and you're not stupid.'

She managed a smile.

'You've got two choices,' he said gently. 'Walk away or stay. If you stay it will get worse before it gets better. If you walk away now, before you're any further involved, there's a chance you can get your life back. Maybe even do something different.'

He paused and added, 'It's an easy choice, when you think about it.'

'What about you, though? Do you have that choice?'

He shook his head. 'It's too late for me. I've got to sort out my part in this business, if I walk away now, this thing will just follow me.'

She nodded. 'That makes it easy.'

'It does?'

She smiled at him. 'I'm staying, too,' she said. 'Remember?'

They could have got out and made a run for it even then. They might even have got away with it and survived. But they didn't. They stayed. Jake wanted to bring things to a head.

It was a long, slow morning. Dawn had been and gone. Nothing had happened. Sunrise arrived. Nothing happened. The day wore on, a dull, murky sort of day.

'Maybe they don't know we're here?' Anna suggested.

'They know.'

They must have been close to panic in the early hours, he thought.

Another body to dispose of without arousing concern. Another hiccup in their programme.

They would have looked for him in the village. Then they would come out here to the cottage. When they saw the car they wouldn't be able to believe their luck; they had him cornered, Anna as well.

Dixie would be an unsettling puzzle, though. The unknown woman who had rescued Anna and shot their man. Who the hell was she?

'When do you think they'll come?' Anna asked, breaking into his thoughts.

He shook his head. 'They'll be looking to wear us down. So they'll come when they think we'll least expect them, hoping we'll be tired and careless.'

'I thought you said they would come with first light?'

'Military style would be to come before first light. Launch the attack under cover of darkness. Get into position, at least.'

'But they didn't, did they?'

He shook his head.

'What does that tell you? They're not military?'

He knew what she was doing. She was keeping the talking going. She wanted to believe he knew what he was doing, that he was the expert she needed him to be. He didn't mind that. He understood. She didn't have the experience. He did.

'We know they're not military,' he said gently. 'What they are is clever and ruthless. And highly motivated.'

'They're keeping us guessing,' she said. 'Maybe they won't come at all?'

'They'll come.'

He was sure of that, if not much else. There was a lot at stake for them. Whoever they were. Everything, in fact.

But it had been a long morning, and it looked set to be a long day.

Jake mostly watched the back of the house and the hillside beyond. Anna circulated.

'They won't come now, will they?' she asked. 'Not in broad daylight.'

He shrugged. 'They might, if they want to surprise us. But you're probably right.'

Why come in broad daylight, with all the extra dangers that would entail? Unless something had happened to slow them down. Like not having enough men left standing. Attrition must have taken some toll.

'They must have been delayed?' Anna suggested.

He nodded. He watched as she fiddled with the useless mobile, and then with the gun Dixie had loaned her. She wasn't used to being in the field. She hadn't learned how to conserve her energy. She hadn't learned patience.

'How did you get into this game?' he asked.

'What, you think I'm not good enough?'

'Of course not,' he said hastily.

She chuckled. 'Of course you do. I'm not like Dixie.'

'Nobody's like Dixie. Nobody in the world.'

She wanted to talk. He didn't mind. Some of the pressure and urgency had faded as the day wore on.

'I was in the Guides when I was at school,' she said quietly. 'This seemed a natural progression after university.'

'That all?'

She nodded.

'Why don't I believe you?'

'It's true!'

'But you've left something out.'

She grinned. 'Quite a lot, actually.'

'Family history play a part?'

'I guess it did. My dad was something special in the Armed Forces. I idolized him.'

He said nothing. He could guess the rest. The important part, at least.

'He was killed on active service,' she said quietly. 'I thought my own life had ended, too.'

'How old were you then?'

'Fifteen. Fifteen and a quarter.'

He nodded. She'd had no real choice after that. She'd had to do something special herself.

'You could have worn a uniform,' he pointed out.

'Yes. And no doubt done very well. But I chose this instead. In fact, it pretty well chose me.'

'Any reason?'

'I thought I'd be good at it.' She flashed him a grin and added, 'I'm a clever girl, see!'

He smiled and turned back to the window. She was right. She wasn't like Dixie. She liked talking, and talking helped her. She wasn't like Dixie at all.

About ten o'clock a big 4by4 appeared on the track leading to the cottage. Anna spotted it first. She called him.

'It's stopped,' she added. Then : 'Recognise it?'

He peered through the window and shook his head. Black. Dark windows. Quite a lot of chrome. Made in Japan, he guessed, or South Korea. He wasn't very good at cars. Not that its origin mattered. It just sat there, like a huge dung beetle. Only this one was seeking to intimidate.

'It's them, isn't it?' Anna whispered.

'Yep.'

It would be them, whoever "them" was.

'So they're coming,' she added.

'Not yet.' He shook his head. 'They're trying to unnerve us, or else it's a distraction.'

'Maybe they're just trying to keep us locked in?'

'Maybe. Another possibility is they're waiting for reinforcements. They're a couple of men down, remember.'

She considered that and nodded. 'So what do you want to do?'

'Nothing.'

She glanced at him.

'At the moment. Just keep your eye on it. I'll watch the other side, in case it's a feint.'

She gave him an uncertain smile. 'We'll be all right, won't we?'

'Of course we will!'

He grinned and hoped he was right. It had become them or us. When they arrived, it would be with all guns blazing. They wouldn't be coming to take prisoners. Not now. They were past the stage when that might have been a possibility.

Right now though they were just letting them know they were here. As if! he thought with a wry smile, as if we didn't know already.

The phone began to ring. The landline. They looked at each other. Jake shrugged and went to pick it up.

'You have a choice,' a voice said.

'And what might that be?'

'Come out now, hands on heads.'

'Or?'

'Or face the consequences.'

'Some choice.'

'It's what you have.'

He didn't recognize the speaker's voice. Not that he would have expected to.

He didn't recognize the choice either.

'So?' the voice asked.

'My answer isn't original.'

'Go on.'

'Nuts.'

'That it?'

'Yeah.'

'Think you're as good a man as General Patton?'

'We'll have to see, won't we?'

'We surely will.'

The line went dead again.

'What did you say?' Anna asked, looking puzzled.

'Nuts.'

She just shook her head. He wasn't sure she approved.

'It's what General Patton said when the Germans offered him surrender terms during the Battle of the Bulge.'

'That was before I was born,' she said, looking away. 'You can't expect me to know everything.'

CHAPTER TWENTY-NINE

Nothing seemed to be happening on the hillside at the back of the cottage. He didn't really expect anything. Unless they were seriously pressed for time they wouldn't come yet. They would use surprise as a weapon. Doing what they imagined to be unexpected was what they were trained to do. They were just putting on a show at the moment. Possibly while they waited for reinforcements.

'The car's gone!' Anna called.

He went to verify it. The track was empty.

Anna looked up at him.

'They'll be back,' he said.

Just then his mobile rang. He saw Anna staring at him wide-eyed as he answered it.

'Want me to follow them?' Dixie asked.

'It's up to you but don't frighten them off. We need them.'

Dixie laughed and switched off.

'*That* mobile works,' Anna said reprovingly. 'And hers.'

'Sat phones,' he said.

'I wonder what else you haven't told me,' she said, turning away.

Jake wondered about Anna's boss, Ed Donaldson. What was he up to? And . . . well, who was he?

'He's pretty new,' Anna said. 'Not to the work. To the job, I mean. He used to be somewhere else. I don't know where.'

'In Five, you mean?'

'I don't know.'

'So he runs a team, does he?'

'He's a pretty senior guy, but don't ask me, Jake. I shouldn't be talking to you about internal stuff.'

'We don't know much about him, do we?' he mused. 'We don't know why he's got such a down on me either.'

'Maybe he just doesn't want to be distracted from his main responsibility.'

'Maybe. But how come he was taking such a direct role with you? Junior staff – with all due respect – wouldn't normally come under senior management.'

'It's a new approach he's introduced – mentoring. Each senior person has a direct link with at least one junior person.'

Jake said nothing.

'It keeps the senior people in touch with the shop floor,' she continued. 'And it helps junior staff development, as well.'

Still he said nothing.

'It's a philosophy Ed brought with him from his old place, wherever that was. Most of us like it. I think it's good,' she added defiantly.

'What does middle management think?'

'Oh, some of them are not keen. I guess it reduces their own role.'

'Is there someone else you could talk to? Someone in middle management, perhaps?'

She was about to object. Then she stopped herself. 'You think we may be able to find out more about what's going on?'

'It's a possibility. Even more about Ed Donaldson might help. What do you think?'

'I'm not supposed to go outside the loop.'

'Of course not.'

She thought about it. What did it matter anyway? As if she wasn't already way outside the loop. As he watched her, it didn't seem worth reminding her where she was now.

'There's Bob Simpson, I suppose.'

'Bob Simpson?'

'My immediate boss. He sort of likes me,' she added, with a wry smile.

'I'm sure he does.'

'I could ask him.'

'Why don't you? He sounds just the man.'

'It's not what you think,' she said with a grin.

'Oh, I bet it is!'

Later, she said, 'Who's the painter?'

'Me.'

'Did you do that one?' she asked, nodding towards a big blue watercolour of a dragonfly in flight that occupied a prominent position on the wall.

He nodded.

'And the others, in the spare bedroom?'

'Yes, those, as well.'

She nodded thoughtfully.

Suddenly he felt defensive. Until Anna and Dixie had arrived, no-one else had seen any of his pictures. And Dixie hadn't noticed them. At least, she hadn't said anything.

'It's a hobby,' he said. 'That's all.'

She nodded again.

'I mean, I'm not an artist or anything. I'm untrained.'

'Self-taught?' she asked.

'It shows, doesn't it?'

She walked away from him. He shrugged. He wasn't going to cry about it.

'This one's terrific,' she said over her shoulder, gazing at the dragonfly painting.

He waited.

'I mean it,' she said. 'This is wonderful. I really like it.'

He tried to laugh, but somehow he couldn't. He was touched.

'This painting,' she added, 'makes me feel as if I'm on the edge of a world I know next to nothing about. Is that why you paint insects?'

He shrugged. 'I guess so. That's the point of it – life on the moor.'

'You're a really sensitive man, aren't you? Underneath that tough exterior.'

'Let's hope I'm still as tough as I used to think I was,' he said, turning away.

But he'd seen the look on her face, the thoughtful look that said she was seeing him in a different light. It made him feel good about himself. Better, anyway.

He felt rather than heard her come into the room. He didn't turn round. He was watching two sheep with their heads up.

'Anything?' she asked softly.

'Probably not.'

He sensed her moving across the floor. The air stirred behind him. She didn't make a sound. Her scent came to him.

The sheep moved. One opened its mouth and called, more a croak than a bleat. The bracken swayed and two other, younger sheep tumbled out into the open. Grown-up lambs which had not yet entirely left their mothers. Nothing to worry about.

'What are you studying?' she asked, moving up close behind him.

He pointed out the scene.

'The sheep?'

She leaned over his shoulder to peer out of the window, her body suddenly inches from his.

'I wondered if something had disturbed them,' he said, trying to remain calm and off-hand about her proximity. 'But they're happy enough now.'

She rested a hand on his shoulder and he felt her weight as she leaned further forward to peer in all directions.

'We'll be all right for a while,' he said, his mouth gone dry. 'They won't come in daytime. Not now.'

'No?'

'No. They'll wait for darkness now, having waited this long.'

He turned his head to look up at her. His face accidentally met her breast, soft and yet firm beneath the satin of her clothing. He drew back with a start from the warmth. He hadn't realized she was quite that close.

'Sorry.'

She said nothing but she didn't pull away either. She gazed down at him.

'What?' she said after a moment.

'Your perfume,' he said, improvising.

'Don't you like it?'

'Love it,' he said, smiling, trying to recover. 'But you can't use stuff like that in the field. I didn't hear you enter the room but I picked up your scent as soon as you moved.'

'Ever the consummate professional,' she whispered, straightening up and gazing at him now with evident amusement.

He gazed back at her. Their eyes met and locked. Suddenly she shivered and reached out to him. He felt her arms go round his neck. She pressed herself against him, her belly against his face. He put his arms round her and pulled her even closer.

He felt the heat of her against his face. He closed his eyes for a moment. Then he drew back and reached up. He drew her down on top of him, cushioning her on the floor. Her lips found his. She kissed him hard. He pulled her even closer.

She pushed back and sat up. He helped her pull her shirt over her head. She unhooked her bra. He pulled it away and buried his face in her breasts as they swung free. He felt her pulling at his belt, unfastening it.

He rolled her over on to her back. She didn't seem to notice the hard floor, covered only by the thin rug. She spread her legs. His fingers found her moist already and he entered her very quickly. They made love urgently. For a time they disappeared into one another. For a time nothing else mattered.

Afterwards he held her silently. She clung to him like a survivor. He was her hope, her only hope.

'I'm glad,' she said eventually. 'About this. You and me.'

'So am I,' he told her.

'It had to happen, didn't it?'

'From the moment I first saw you.'

He meant it, all of it. She laughed and hugged him hard. He smiled back. It would be all right. He knew that now.

CHAPTER THIRTY

'So who was she?' Anna asked softly.

Jake looked up. 'Give me a clue,' he responded, but he knew what she meant.

'You don't have to tell me, of course.'

'Don't I?'

'You could be in denial.'

'I don't know what you're talking about.'

'No, of course you don't.'

They looked out of different windows for a while, without seeing anything.

'It might help,' Anna said.

Jake tussled with it.

'Did Dixie know her?'

Maybe she was right to ask? Maybe it was time, time to get it out in the open. Three years was long enough. He knew now he couldn't stay here for the rest of his life, living on memories and drinking from such a bitter cup. He'd known that for a while, and even more surely for the past several days. Once the adrenaline had started to flow, he'd become a different person. His old self again and he felt better for it.

'You're doing nothing here, Jake. You're wasting your life. Why?'

It was hard to admit it but she was probably right about that too. Time to move on, before it was too late. Dixie already had, of course. A long time ago. He'd tried to himself, but he'd gone in the wrong direction. He knew that now. He'd been alone too long.

'Ellie,' he said.

'She died, didn't she?'

He nodded, surprised how easy it was to admit it.

Then he told her.

He looked up as Anna came back into the room. He smiled. She smiled back. How well they got on together, he thought. And how surprising that was.

'You look pleased with yourself,' he said.

'So I am.' She handed him back his sat phone. 'I've just been talking to one of my many admirers.'

'I'll kill him.'

She laughed. 'Step back! Owen is too nice for that.'

'Owen? He's not Welsh, is he?'

'Scottish, actually.'

'That doesn't sound right.'

'No. He blames his mother.'

'Mothers, eh? They can cause a lot of trouble.'

'Don't get me started on that subject, Jake. Anyway, I couldn't reach Bob Simpson but I had a really interesting chat with Owen. Learned a few things about Ed.'

He looked at her and waited expectantly.

'First, Owen doesn't like him, or trust him. Hates him, in fact.'

'That's not an abnormal attitude towards your boss. Especially if he's just arrived and wants to turn things upside-down.'

'It's more than that.' She shook her head. 'Owen says Ed is very anti-Scots.'

'Normal.'

'And very reactionary. He doesn't approve of the Scottish Parliament, or the disproportionately great influence of Scottish MPs in Westminster. Never mind Scottish independence! Owen doesn't like any of that.'

'Again. . . .'

'And when Ed moved into Five, guess where he came from?'

Jake said nothing for a moment. Then he frowned. 'Go on,' he urged.

'Six!'

Jake was stunned.

'Isn't that a surprise?'

He blew out explosively and nodded. 'A big surprise,' he admitted. 'It's hard to believe.'

There wasn't a lot of movement between the two services, either at operational nor senior level. They had different cultures and different purposes. Different loyalties, too. They were intense rivals.

'Maybe,' he said slowly, 'the real reason why Owen doesn't trust him is because he's come from the other side.'

'Perhaps. I think that's only part of it. There are other reasons. When he came, he brought some people with him. A tight little cadre of henchmen. Like when a football manager changes clubs, and goes back to his old club to fetch all his favourite players and coaches. Does that happen a lot?' Anna quizzed.

'In the Service?' Jake shook his head. 'I've never heard of such a thing. What do they do, these guys from Six?'

'Owen doesn't know. They work only with Ed. Something special, he says. Something out of the ordinary.'

'It must be. Your Department must have been in a hell of a state to put up with that.'

'It was, I think. The recent surge of terrorism; 9/11 and the bombings in London, as well as other scares, revealed how threadbare Five really was. It showed how under-staffed, poorly qualified and inexperienced we were, as well.

'So we've expanded massively. We're tailing thousands of suspects now. And you need a lot of people for that. We didn't have them. We didn't have the languages or cultural skills either.'

'That might have been where Six came in,' Jake said slowly. 'If Five had wanted more Arabic speakers, Six would have been a good place to go for them.'

He wondered why his and Ed Donaldson's paths had never crossed. Their world hadn't been that big. Boxes, he supposed. Separate boxes. They were all in their little boxes; not so much comfort zones, more an elementary precaution. It was of damage limitation, in the event of things going wrong. This way there was only so much an operative could give away, whatever the form of torture used.

He wondered if he'd got it wrong, after all. Could Donaldson be legitimate? Perhaps the likes of him and Rogers were more the norm than he'd always thought; both seemed to have prospered.

'So, really,' he suggested, 'this business up here must be a right nuisance to him. If Donaldson's got all this on his plate, he's not going to want to spend precious time and resources on a royal visit to some piddling little village in Northumberland. He's got much bigger and more pressing problems to sort out.'

'I'm sure that's right,' Anna admitted. 'It's probably why he involved me. I could be spared.'

'In fact, the wonder is that he bothered with any of this at all. Why on earth not just leave it all to the Met, and their Royal Protection team?'

'He's very conscientious.'

'He must be.'

'He wouldn't renege on an agreement or not carry out something he'd promised.'

'Like what, for example?'

'Well, it was part of my training programme, wasn't it?' she said defensively. 'He's committed to this mentoring idea, and he wouldn't give up on it just because he was busy.'

Jake gave her a speculative look. 'Do you really believe that?'

'No,' she said with a shrug.

'Good. Neither do I.'

'There's something else. Owen says the word is that Ed isn't going to be the next DG.'

'Oh? That's too bad.'

'He's got political backing, apparently, and he's destined for even higher things.'

'I can't believe I'm hearing this.'

'I believe it. Owen says he's been brought across for a couple of years for the experience and the insight. That's why he's brought a team with him. Then they're going to make him the next Chairman of the Joint Intelligence Committee.'

Jake just stared.

'Owen says that's the story. He believes it and says that's how it will be.'

'Why?'

'New broom! The theory is that because he hasn't been DG of either of them, he'll be better placed to weigh one up against the other. Besides, they think he's good.'

'They must do,' Jake said heavily.

Cedric had told him something similar about someone else recently. He wondered how Donaldson and Rogers would get on together – not at all well, was his guess!

There seemed to be a lot of them about these days, rising stars. The rivalry must be intense. Not like in his day. Terrible events had once again proved a fertile spawning ground. The people who let off bombs had no idea what they were doing.

He wondered if there might be a way of playing Donaldson and Rogers off against one other. That would be nice. Proving the old theory again. Two negatives making a positive.

CHAPTER THIRTY-ONE

The light faded fast. There was a burst of fire in the west, above the Cheviots, and then clouds streamed across the sky and darkness came to the valley and the hillside.

Jake was undecided. He stood outside, by the back door of the cottage, studying the sky and weighing their options. The heavy overcast weather made a difference. There was no moonlight or starlight; it would be a black night. There was rain in the air, as well. He could smell it. That made even more of a difference, although the change cut both ways. They wouldn't be able to see him any better than he could see them.

Still, the advantage would be with the other side. It would be impossible to see them coming on a night like tonight was shaping up to be. They could be into the house before he or Anna knew it. Dixie wouldn't be able to see or do much either. If she was still around. So the cottage was more of a trap now than a safe refuge. It was time to move.

Anna was still at her post by an upstairs window.

'Get your stuff together,' he said quietly. 'We're moving out.'

He saw the white blur of her face as she turned to him.

'What stuff?'

He shrugged. She had a point.

'What are you thinking, Jake?'

'It's dark now, and going to be darker. Rain's on the way, as well. It's going to be a black night.'

'So we'll not see them coming?'

He nodded. 'Our chances will be better outside.'

'What about Dixie? She won't know what's going on.'

He shrugged. 'Dixie will cope. I have confidence in her.'

She stared hard at him. 'You must have,' she said heavily.

'We go back a long way, Dixie and me.'

'You don't have to explain, Jake,' she said, getting to her feet.

'Not in that way,' he said, looking to repair any possible damage. 'We're just friends.'

'Friends, right.'

'Good friends – and colleagues. That's all.'

'I see,' she said, reaching for the fleece he'd given her.

'I'll find you a better jacket,' he said. 'One that will keep you dry.'

She didn't reply. She moved away from him.

Why the hell did it have to be so complicated? he wondered as he left the room.

He began to tell her in detail what she should do. She stopped him. 'I know what to do, Jake.'

'Of course you do. What was I thinking?'

'You don't need to worry about me. I may not be Dixie, but I know what to do. I have been trained.'

He nodded. Time would tell.

'Stick close, then,' he told her. 'Let's find out where they are first, and how many they are.'

The rain had begun ten minutes earlier. Now it was gathering pace, beginning to drum on the roof and rattle the windows. With it had come a gusty wind. For a moment he watched the raindrops hitting the iron-hard ground and bouncing upwards in a series of miniature explosions. More like a summer thunderstorm than an autumn shower. It made their move even more urgent.

He held on to the kitchen door firmly as he ushered Anna outside. She slipped past him and crossed the yard. She waited by the wall of the old outhouse as he made sure the door was shut firmly behind him. Old habits, he thought ruefully. He doubted the expected visitors would take such care.

He reached her in the shadows and stooped to kiss her cheek. She clutched his arm for a moment and pressed her head against his chest. Then he pulled away and set off to lead the way up the hillside behind the house. He stuck to one of the many sheep tracks that crossed the close-nibbled turf and ran through the waving, already-sodden bracken. They didn't go far before slipping into a small hollow overlooking the cottage. They settled there and began to wait. The rain was falling heavily now, slanting across the blackness to patter on the bracken all around them.

Jake tried to ignore the water streaming across his face, but from time to time he needed to blink hard and wipe his eyes with his fingers. He sheltered the shotgun as best he could with his jacket.

After an hour he began to have some misgivings. Niggling doubts set in. He wondered whether he'd got it right. Even if they did come, wouldn't the noise of the wind and rain screen any sounds of movement?

They would come, he told himself. They would come. All he and Anna had to do was watch and wait.

But on a night like this? Maybe they had just parked their vehicle on the track to hold them down, intimidate them?

No, they must come. They would see the weather as a godsend. Apart from anything else, they were running out of time. And for some reason he still couldn't see, they wanted him out of the way before the action began. They seemed to need to clear the decks.

Anna nudged his arm with her elbow. Then she gently turned his head with her hand and pointed him to the left of the cottage. He stared and got it. Movement. He tap-tapped her arm. It was starting.

Two, three figures? He wasn't sure.

They watched as the movement drew nearer the cottage. Jake readied the shotgun. It wasn't a match for automatic weapons, but it wasn't useless either. Nor was the handgun Dixie had loaned Anna.

He squinted hard into the wet darkness, intent on the blurry figures, ghosts in the night moving forward quickly. One of them was bent almost double. They passed into a deeper pool of shadow and he lost the outline of their figures. They became just a hint of movement, getting ever closer to the cottage. Moving more cautiously.

It was impossible to see much more, or to do anything from this range, hard even to know where they were. It would be a bit of a lottery in this light, but at least the rain was easing and the wind had dropped. Still he hesitated.

Then suddenly night became day. With a dull thump the 4by4 on the track erupted in a sheet of flame that illuminated the cottage and the entire hillside beyond. A hot wind scorched his face. Smoke, sparks and debris cascaded over their heads.

Jake stared, wide-eyed. Anna gasped and clutched his arm.

'Dixie!' he said after a moment, turning to her with a grin. 'The fuel tank.'

He turned back again. The light was fading almost as fast as it had appeared.

'Three of them!' he snapped, spotting the exposed figures below them.

The figures were closer now. Only thirty yards below their own position, they were standing upright now, in consternation – gesticulating and shouting.

Jake clambered to his feet. Then a second explosion, and a third and a fourth, stopped him momentarily. But these were different. Less powerful. Not so much light. Different source.

He realised what was happening. The figures below were hurling grenades into the cottage. Stun grenades. And smoke grenades. Flames erupted inside the house. Black smoke billowed through the kitchen window. He heard the chatter of automatic weapons. Nothing subtle about this attack. And nothing was being left to chance. They were up against the clock now.

His cottage, though!

Fury dispelled caution. He set off fast down the slope. A face turned towards him when he was half-way there. He fired the shotgun one-handed, by then at almost point-blank range. The figure screamed, reeled and dropped.

Another figure appeared at a kitchen window. A fast tap-tap from somewhere off to his side brought it tumbling through the window. Anna! he realized with surprise and approval. One to her.

The third? He'd seen three. There could be more.

He jogged round the side of the cottage. A body lay crumpled on the ground. He kicked it. Dead. He didn't know how or why. He paused and stood upright, taking stock.

Movement caught his eye, and a beam of light. A figure, another figure, was sauntering down the track towards the cottage, wielding a torch and whistling. Whistling for the Confederacy.

Jake breathed out and stood waiting, using the time to re-load, the fury dissipating, calm returning.

'I might have known,' he said conversationally. 'Is that all of them?'

'All of them they sent here,' Dixie said. 'There's another one next to the jeep.'

She came up close.

'Thanks,' he said. 'I particularly liked the pyrotechnics. That was a nice touch.'

Dixie shrugged modestly. Then stepped sideways and peered past him. 'What's she doing?'

He spun round to see Anna emerge from the cottage, coughing and spluttering. There was bright light behind her now. The flames inside had taken hold. Anna doubled over, retching. He set off to jog towards her.

'I'm sorry, Jake,' she gasped as he drew near. 'I thought I might be able to do something, but . . . I just got this.'

She broke off, coughing some more, and lowered something she was carrying to the ground. He saw it was the painting, the dragonfly painting, the one she'd liked so much. He reached out to hug her.

'The cottage, Jake!' Dixie said.

He glanced across and knew it was hopeless. It was too late. There was nothing anyone could do now to quench the flames.

They moved back, away from the growing heat, and watched in silence for a few moments.

'Is there anything you really need to reach in there?' Dixie asked.

He shook his head and turned his back on the inferno. There was nothing worth going back for. It had been his home for three years, but soon it would be a pile of ashes and nothing more. That would be it.

They checked the four bodies but found nothing personal or identifiable on them. They were just bodies. Dead bodies.

'Professionals,' Dixie said, as if there had still been any doubt.

Jake nodded. 'Let's go,' he said. 'We're running out of time.'

'But they're running out of men, as well as time,' Dixie pointed out.

'Yeah. Let's go.'

'Where?' Anna wheezed, breaking off to cough hard. 'Where are we going?'

Jake didn't answer. He set off along the track.

CHAPTER THIRTY-TWO

From Cedric's house it was possible to see much of the main street. Not the new social housing development, which was on the same side of the road, and therefore out of sight, but most of the buildings from which there would be a clear view of the entrance to the development – and a clear shot at someone preparing to enter it.

Cedric, revealing little surprise at their appearance, despite the hour, or at their number, showed them into the attics.

'Help yourselves,' he said, 'to anything you can find. This is a self-contained flat, a holiday flat we let out. So you'll find just about everything you need here. There's even some food in the fridge.'

He said little else, obviously feeling it wasn't the moment, and turned to leave. He didn't even wait to be introduced.

Jake followed him out on to the landing. 'Sorry about dumping ourselves on you like this, Ced.'

'I knew you were in some sort of trouble,' Cedric said with a grin, 'but *two* ladies?'

'At my age, as well? I know, I know!' Jake shook his head. 'It's just for a day or two. It'll be over then, one way or another.'

'Is there anything else I can do, Jake? I mean it.'

He sounded more like the old Cedric, the man Jake had come to count as a friend. Still Jake shook his head, though. 'You've done enough, Ced. This is serious. They burned my cottage down tonight.'

Cedric stared and then said, 'Who did?'

'People who are no longer with us.'

Cedric nodded and turned away.

'I could do with a hand-gun, Ced. Is the offer still open?'

'Of course.'

Cedric led the way downstairs and into the storeroom behind the shop. 'I take it there's nothing more you want to tell me?'

'Just keep your head down, mate. That's all I can say at the moment.'

It was all he wanted to say. He had come here only because at short notice he couldn't think of anywhere better. Instinct told him to be cautious. The business in the Narrow Nick coming so soon after visiting Cedric wasn't forgotten, nor was the mystery of Caitlin's whereabouts.

'Is it about the Royal visit?' Cedric pressed.

Jake nodded. 'Probably. How did you know?' he asked with an ironic smile.

'Inspired guess!' Cedric said with a wry chuckle.

Dixie was not good indoors. She fretted. She got to feel claustrophobic. Her cheeks flushed. She grew hot. She pulled with an air of growing distraction at the neck line of her T-shirt. Jake recognised the signs. Remembered them from their time together. Now she'd had a couple of hours rest, she ached to be away again before first light.

'One of us should be outside, Dixie,' he said carefully. 'We need to know what's happening on the street.'

'Me, you mean?'

'I was thinking that, yes.'

'So you can be cosy with her?'

He was taken aback, shocked even. There was an unexpected note of bitterness in her voice. He stared at her.

Dixie was unrepentant. 'You've had her in the sack, haven't you?'

'Come on, Dixie!'

'Haven't you?'

He just stared at her.

'Miss Wonderful!' she said scornfully. 'Doesn't know her ass from her elbow.'

He didn't respond. Instead, they circled round one another. He picked things up and put them back down again. She stared out the window.

'Ellie would understand,' he said eventually, 'if that's what's bothering you. I can't live like a monk forever.'

She glared at him a moment longer. Then she turned and began collecting a few things together.

With dismay he suddenly realized it might not have anything to do with what Ellie might have thought.

'You and I were never possible, Dixie,' he said gently. 'Not in that way. You know that. There never was that spark between us.'

'Forget it, Jake.'

'If anything had been meant to happen between us, it would have. A long time ago.'

'Forget it! OK?'

'You think I brought you here under false pretences?'

'I think nothing. I'm out of here.'

'If you're leaving, Dixie, I understand. I don't want you to go, but—'

'I'm going to check out the backs of the buildings opposite. One of us should. I'll let you know what I find.'

He nodded.

Moments later she was gone.

He grimaced and felt bad. He was just using Dixie, he supposed; not surprisingly, she resented it.

How had he been to know? How was he supposed to realize she thought their relationship was different to the way he saw it?

He should have known. After all this time, he should have, but he hadn't. Not really.

He returned to the window and waited for Anna to come back from her shower. It was dark still – quite black. He wondered if the flames had died out yet in his cottage. He wondered what was left of it. Anything? The foundations, probably. Not much more. What a waste.

Nothing moved out on the street. There were no lights in any of the buildings opposite. And just one pale street light was still lit. He saw nothing of Dixie. He hadn't expected to.

She was a strange one, and seemed stranger now than ever. Thinking back, he supposed she had always behaved as if they were closer than they actually were. There had been intimacy, of a sort, but it hadn't been physical. Somehow it had never got that far. Always there had been something holding them apart. He had never worked out what it was: religious values; inexperience – a kind of innocence; a distaste for physical contact – revulsion even; sexual identity, perhaps? He really didn't know. After all this time, he still didn't know.

But something had always got in the way. Then Ellie had come on the scene, and for him everything had been wonderfully straightforward and clear after that. Dixie had seemed to accept it graciously. She might even have been secretly relieved.

Now what was he to think? He swore and stared harder out of the window. Now he should forget it, he told himself. There were more urgent matters to address.

He heard Anna come back into the room from the shower but he didn't look round immediately.

'Where's Dixie?' he heard her say.

'Gone. She's on the outside.'

'Good!'

He turned then with surprise, ready to rebuke her, and was in time to see her drop the bath towel and stand still, and naked, smiling at him.

Her breasts swayed gently, invitingly, and for the moment he forgot about Dixie and her problems, real or imagined.

'We have time, don't we?' Anna said innocently.

He didn't even bother to reply as he moved to meet her, not daring to trust himself to speak.

CHAPTER THIRTY-THREE

The car was a highly-polished, black Volvo, an executive model of some sort, no doubt with an extraordinary engine beneath the gleaming metal. Jake watched it manoeuvre into position on the flat bench beside the river. From his perch on Shilhope Law he could see it well.

'Now get out,' he instructed on his mobile. 'And open all the doors.'

The driver's door opened and a man got out. He walked slowly around the car, opening doors. Without being told to he also opened the boot.

Jake scanned the car with his binoculars and was satisfied. It was empty. Nor was there any other vehicle in sight. He got to his feet and set off down the hill. The man standing beside the car spotted him and watched for a moment. Then he began shutting the car doors. But he didn't get back inside. He seemed to understand that that wouldn't be acceptable.

'And you are. . . ?' the man called as Jake approached him.

'Jake Ord.'

'Bob Cunningham. Northumbria Police Special Branch.'

A name but no rank. Jake guessed Special Branches everywhere were like that. Part of the Police Service, but apart. Whatever his rank, Cunningham would report directly to his Chief Constable.

They stood sizing each other up for a moment. Cunningham was slight, a couple of inches under six feet and maybe twelve stone at most – almost willowy. Jake didn't make the mistake of under-estimating him, though. The man was calm and in control, yet brave and prepared to take risks. He was undoubtedly an astute man, too, top-class, in fact, although

Jake was reasonably confident he could take him if it came to a physical contest.

'I should arrest you,' Cunningham said quietly without a smile. 'My colleagues are unhappy with you.'

'Try it.'

'I still might.' He gave Jake a very direct stare and then said, 'What have you got for me?'

'You know who I am, and what I was?'

'I know.'

That saved time.

'You've got trouble. So have I. Several attempts have been made in recent days to kill me. A former colleague living nearby was killed a few days' ago. The wife of another one is being held hostage. There are people – rogue officers from the Security Service, I believe – planning the assassination of the Prince of Wales when he's here on Friday.

'A very senior guy in MI5 is at least partly responsible for some of this. Perhaps totally responsible. Six of his people are dead, and he's spirited the bodies away from under the noses of officers from the Met without them doing anything about it. And a snatch squad tried unsuccessfully to take out a current, more junior MI5 operative.'

'And you evaded arrest.'

Jake nodded.

Cunningham waited a moment and then said, 'Anything else?'

'A few details. My cottage was burned down last night, for instance.'

The other man raised his eyebrows and then nodded. 'My Chief Constable won't be happy about that. We already have a housing shortage in this area. Too many properties becoming holiday cottages. Local youngsters find it very difficult to get on the housing ladder these days.'

'I'm not happy about it either.'

Cunningham turned and gazed up the valley. 'Beautiful country, this,' he said. 'I used to camp around here when I was a boy. I loved it.'

'That right?'

'Father was a shepherd. Not here, though. Over in the Ingram Valley, a bit further north. But Uncle Billy had the farm at Meckendon for a time.'

Jake waited.

'You like it here yourself?' Cunningham asked.

'Better than anywhere else I've been.'

Cunningham nodded again. He paused a moment, seemingly lost in thought, and then said, 'I'll see what I can do.'

Jake felt hope stirring for the first time.

'My Chief Constable takes a dim view of London battles being fought on his patch, especially on his watch.'

Jake waited.

'What do you think I should do?'

'Cancel the Royal visit and arrest Donaldson. That would be a good start.'

Cunningham sat down on a rock, and waved Jake to do the same. 'Let's hear the details,' he suggested.

It took a while even to give him the edited version, which was all that Jake was prepared to disclose at that point. Cunningham listened intently, occasionally asking for clarification of a point. Jake felt he was getting somewhere.

'We work with the Met in a situation like this,' Cunningham said thoughtfully. 'They have lead responsibility, but we still have a big interest.'

Jake felt there was no need for him to sit there being told the obvious, but he didn't say so. The man had a lot to get his head around.

'Grainger and Collins, you say? It would be hard trying to tell the Met their men were running amok, even if it were true.'

He looked directly at Jake, who shrugged and kept quiet. 'In fact, who would we tell? Grainger's a top man. And the MI5 guy he's liaising with is also a top man. In fact, I understand he's second only to their DG.'

Jake kept a straight face. 'These things happen,' he said.

'My Chief Constable is not going to like any little bit of this – if I tell him.'

Jake could see that. He stirred. 'Bob, I brought you the problem. I didn't say I had the solution.'

Cunningham smiled for the first time. 'It's a wild story, young man.'

'Isn't it? How do you think I feel? A week ago I was living in romantic seclusion in my cottage on the moor. Now I'm a . . . a fugitive!'

Cunningham got to his feet.

'So what are you going to do?' Jake asked.

'Check things out. Stay in touch, you've got my number.'

'And you've got mine,' Jake reminded him, 'but there isn't much time.'

Cunningham nodded and got back into his car. He didn't ask Jake if he wanted a lift.

Jake watched the car disappear. Then his phone vibrated. He took it out and answered.

'What did he say?' Dixie asked.

'He's going to think about it.'

'Man of action, eh?'

'He's OK, I think.'

'Good. We need some help.'

'What about Caitlin? Any progress?'

'I'm working on it.'

CHAPTER THIRTY-FOUR

'They've got her at a farm, Jake.'

'Where?'

'Near a place called Kirknewton.'

He knew the area. It was about as remote as you could get in north Northumberland without going into Scotland.

'How do you know?'

'I followed them.'

Stupid question. She'd followed them. He didn't bother asking how she'd managed that.

'How many people are holding her?'

'I'm not sure, I've just got here. Two or three, I think. Do you want me to get her out?'

He thought fast. Dixie could possibly get her out, but there just might be more to contend with at the farm than she knew – better to be safe.

'Wait for me, Dixie. I'm coming.'

'How long will you be?'

'An hour. No more.'

Kirknewton wasn't much. There were a few scattered houses and a couple of barns; an old school building, now disused; a modern school building, also disused and an ancient church that could have been built by the Angles. In all, a sturdy little hamlet slumbering in the shade of Yeavering Bell, on the northern edge of the Cheviots.

Dixie met him at a local crossroads of four roads going nowhere very much. He stopped the car. She climbed in. He drove a little further and then stopped under some wind-battered sycamores.

'Sheep country,' she said with apparent distaste, wrinkling her nose.

'Nothing wrong with that.'

'Apart from the smell.'

'What? You think cattle don't smell?'

'They smell different.'

He grinned. 'Kind of picky, aren't you? This ain't the nineteenth century, babe. It's not Texas either.'

She grinned back. 'It's pretty nice country, actually. I like it – apart from the sheep smell.'

He took out a 1:50,000 map and opened it. He pronounced the co-ordinates of the farm and stabbed his finger on the spot, 'Cold Acre Farm?'

'That's right.'

It was down in a valley, close to a river although a slight rise put it above the floodplain. A horseshoe-shaped belt of trees protected the farm from winds coming from any direction but the east. There was one road, or track rather, leading into it. A steep hillside rose behind the buildings, on the south side.

'I think this is their main base,' Dixie said. 'This is what we were looking for. And there're more men here than I appreciated initially.'

Jake glanced at her.

'There's been a bit of coming and going since I spoke to you.'

'Getting ready for their big day, I guess.'

Dixie shrugged. 'They're not all guarding Cedric's wife, that's for sure.'

'Any sign of her?'

'Not yet.'

'So we don't really know she's there.'

'She's there,' Dixie said flatly, 'unless she's passed her sell-by-date.'

Sooner or later, Jake thought, she would do just that unless they got her out. So would Cedric. Then good-bye, folks. There would be no further use for them, and they would be a dangerous loose end that needed tidying away. Like himself, of course. If they could find him – and Anna, too. Dixie was safe because they didn't know who the hell she was, or even that she existed.

*

The farm was a mile outside the hamlet. They parked the car next to the old school, beside a couple of tractors and Land Rovers, and set off to walk across fields, following the river. The weather was unsettled now with heavy cloud cover; a blustery wind buffetted them from the north west and rain was in prospect. It looked set to be a good, dark evening ahead for what they had to do.

They studied the farmstead from the lower slopes of the hillside to the south. From that vantage point, they could look over the woodland shelter belt and see the whole place pretty well. There wasn't a lot to it – a house and several low, stone barns, pens for holding the sheep when they were brought down from the hills. There were several cars, no agricultural vehicles, though. Jake guessed the place was now a holiday home rather than a working farm. Donaldson would have rented it. Out of the way, yet close enough to the battlefield. A good choice.

As the light faded and rain began to fall, they worked their way down the slopes, heading for the collection of stone buildings, and hoping Caitlin's value to her captors hadn't been eroded yet.

There was no perimeter guard patrol; Jake assumed they felt safe enough here and that they didn't need it. That there were no dogs either confirmed his impression that it was no longer a working farm. Probably the land was worked by a neighbouring farmer. It was a common enough arrangement these days. You could make more money on a supermarket check-out than as a hill farmer.

They checked the outbuildings systematically, Dixie taking a couple, Jake the others.

'Nothing,' Dixie said when they re-grouped.

'Same here. Everything must be inside the house.'

'Let's go for it,' Dixie suggested.

He nodded. Time to get on, and do what they'd come for.

Keeping to the shadows, they moved swiftly across the yard towards the house. Jake peered upwards at the two storeys. Where would they have her? Not upstairs, surely? No-one would choose to make unnecessary stair climbs all the time. The ground floor, now they were up close, was clearly bigger than it had looked from a distance. It would probably be somewhere at this level, where they could keep an eye on her easily.

Dixie went one way. Jake went the other. The first room he came to was pretty well empty – a store room. Then came a room with bunk beds. Further on a big living room contained an enormous TV, and two men lounging on sofas watching it. The door to this room was shut, he noted, which would be helpful when they went in.

He met Dixie on the far side of the building.

'Four guys,' she whispered. 'In the kitchen. Eating.'

'Four?' That made six they knew about. He grimaced, wondering how many Donaldson had got altogether. It was like a private army. 'What about Caitlin?'

'No sign of her. She must be upstairs.'

If she was here at all. If she was alive. He hoped they hadn't got it wrong.

'Want me to look?' Dixie asked.

He looked up at the wall of the house, which was built in rough Lakeland style, like drystone walling, and therefore good for climbing. He nodded. She was a better climber than him. Lighter and more agile. More in practice, too.

Dixie lowered her backpack to the ground and climbed swiftly to the first window. She came back down and moved to the next window without saying a word. Jake glanced round and followed her.

The same thing.

He began to wonder where else Caitlin could have been stashed. He even wondered if they could have got the whole thing wrong.

Then they found her. Dixie did. She was in a room at the back of the house, a room above the kitchen.

'She's there!' Dixie whispered when she came back down. 'On the bed. Cuffed, I think. Maybe asleep.'

'Anyone with her?'

Dixie shook her head.

He thought fast. They could get in through the window. But could they get Caitlin out the same way? He doubted it. She was too old for gymnastics on walls. Besides, she might have been sedated to keep her quiet.

'Use a rope? Abseil?' Dixie whispered.

He shook his head. Caitlin wouldn't be up to that either. Not without practice. They were going to have to take her out through a door. It didn't matter much whether it was the front door or the back. They would have a fight on their hands either way.

Two of the men in the kitchen finished their meal and left the house, taking a black BMW from the vehicle pool next to the barn. The other two, very domesticated, started washing up.

Jake considered. Only four here now. This might be as good a time as they were going to get.

Dixie climbed back up to the window. Jake waited anxiously while she tapped gently on the glass. She tried again, and again. Then she came back down.

'She can't hear me.'

'Is she alive?'

'She's alive. I saw an arm move.'

That was a relief. She was probably sedated. He thought again and glanced up to the window. It was an old-style wooden sash window, not a hermetically-sealed plastic replacement. No need to smash it.

'We can get that open,' he said. 'Knife blade between the two sashes.'

Dixie nodded. She went back up, and was inside the room in less than a minute. Another minute passed. Then she re-appeared and beckoned him up.

Jake climbed the wall. Not as quickly or as elegantly as Dixie had done, but he did it. He reached the window sill and paused. But by then things had changed. There were four people in the room now.

The two men from the TV room must have finished their programme and come to do their duty. Check on Caitlin. Give her some more sedation, or a toilet break, or whatever.

The timing was sheer hard luck. They'd caught Dixie trying to roust Caitlin. Now there was a gun trained on them both.

'Who the hell are you?' one of the men asked Dixie.

Dixie smiled.

'I'll ask you one more time.'

Dixie stayed where, and as, she was, smiling and silent. Caitlin fidgeted, barely conscious.

'Shut the window,' the guy with the gun said over his shoulder.

His pal came over to the window. Jake ducked. It was now or never. As the man reached up to lower the sash, Jake grabbed a handful of his shirt with one hand and heaved. The other hand he needed to stay on the wall.

The guy didn't want to leave the room. He yelped with shock and pulled back, resisting. Jake let go of the wall, grabbed him with both hands and jerked hard, using all his weight. Both man and window came away then, out into the night in a shower of glass. Jake fell with them. He had no option, but he came off second and somehow landed on top, his fall cushioned.

Just in case, he reached down, grabbed a handful of hair and jerked hard. The guy might well have been dead anyway, but the crack of his neck breaking meant he certainly was now.

Jake hurled himself back at the wall and climbed rapidly, using the temporary flood of adrenaline to get him there, ready to eat bullets if necessary.

Dixie was back on the bed, talking to Caitlin, gently smoothing her face, trying to bring her round. The second man was flat on his back, Dixie's throwing knife in his throat.

'Glad you used my distraction profitably,' he said with relief as he clambered through the gap that had once held the window.

'The door, Jake!' she said urgently.

He was already heading for it, hearing the voices downstairs for himself. On the way, he snatched a gun that had fallen to the floor.

'Harry?' a voice called up the stairs.

Jake glanced down and saw a bulky shape at the foot of the stairs. He ducked back before he heard the boom of a shotgun and felt pieces of wood splintering from the walls and doorway. He dropped flat and waited, but no-one attempted the stairs.

'Caitlin, Caitlin!' he heard Dixie recite as she attempted to restore life to the slumped figure on the bed. 'Come on, come on now!'

And he heard voices below, inside and outside the house. He wondered if there were still just the two guys down there, or if more had appeared. They were safe for the moment, but only for the moment. Somehow they needed to get out – and fast.

He glanced round at Dixie. 'How is she?'

'She'll be fine.'

'How is she now?'

'Alive, but she won't be walking for a while.'

So, he thought, they would be carrying her out. They were trapped for the moment, though, and needed to find an escape route.

'Let's talk?' he called down the stairs.

'So talk!' he heard moments later.

'What are you going to do?' he asked. 'Walk away from here, alive, or stay and take your chances?'

'What about our mate, the one who didn't fall through the window?'

So they knew about that one.

'He didn't make it.'

'No, well neither will you!'

That was what he'd wanted. A second voice. That came from the bottom of the stairs, as well. So they were both inside.

'It was an unfortunate misunderstanding,' Jake said.

He glanced back at Dixie and waved her towards the window. She nodded and stood up. He watched her climb over the sill.

'We can still do a deal,' he called.

'The only deal you can do is come down the stairs now. Hands in the air.'

'This whole thing is a misunderstanding,' Jake suggested, keeping it going. 'When we leave here, I'm going to clear it up.'

'You're not going anywhere, Ord. Come down now or we're ripping this place apart, with you in it.'

He knew they could probably do it, too. They could blow the farmhouse apart with grenades or RPGs. Or just set fire to the place and watch the bodies come tumbling out of the windows.

He winced. Come on, Dixie! What the hell are you doing?

It was quiet now. He'd run out of stupid things to say. So had they, seemingly. Both sides knew no-one would walk away from this.

'Jake?'

He blinked.

'Jake, you can come down now.'

He got to his feet and glanced over at Caitlin. She was awake now. Still groggy, but she smiled at him.

He half-carried her down the stairs and past the two bodies, one at the foot of the stairs, the other in the living room. Quick glances told him Dixie's knife had been busy in one case, and her hands in another. Same old Dixie! he thought with admiration. She'd lost nothing over the years.

'Where are you taking me, Jake?' Caitlin asked sleepily.

'Home, Cait. Home to Cedric.'

'That's good.'

An engine fired in the night. He held Caitlin upright on the front steps and waited in the cool night air for Dixie to bring one of the cars round. It didn't matter which one. Not a lot mattered at that moment. They were alive still. All of them.

CHAPTER THIRTY-FIVE

'You did well, Jake,' Cedric said. 'All of you. Thank you.'

Jake shook his head. 'It shouldn't have come to this.'

'You're right. It shouldn't.'

Nevertheless it had.

'How is she, Ced?'

'Coming round. She'll be fine. Your lady friend is with her at the moment.'

'Anna.'

Cedric smiled, as if a load had been lifted from his shoulders, as indeed it had. 'I'd better get back to her,' he said.

Jake nodded but said nothing more. He watched Cedric go. He reminded himself not to be too hard on the man. He'd been in an impossible situation. Still, he'd lied pretty convincingly at times. It would be hard to trust him again.

Right now, though, there were other things to worry about.

'What do you think, Jake?' Dixie asked.

He shook his head. 'I'm not sure.'

'It's quiet out on the street.'

'Yeah.' He thought about it, wondering what more they could do. 'I'm going to talk some more with Cedric. See what he knows. Then I'm going to call Cunningham.'

'I'll check out a couple of possible sniper positions.'

'Anything yet?'

She shook her head. 'I don't think he's going to come in until the last minute now. But he must have somewhere lined up.'

*

He found Cedric in his study, collapsed rather than relaxed in his chair. Events were taking their toll.

'Cait's sleeping, Jake.'

Jake nodded and planted himself in another chair. 'So what's it all about, Ced?'

'I'm sure you know more than me, Jake.'

'I doubt it. Why did they take Cait?'

'Insurance. Bargaining power.' Cedric shrugged. 'You know how these things work.'

'I'm not sure I do any more. What was the point?'

'To ensure I kept quiet about Sanderson.'

'You're kidding!'

Cedric removed his glasses and rubbed his face with one hand. He looked tired and old. Jake had never seen him look so old.

'They were worried I might speak out about his death.'

'And would you?'

'Possibly. I didn't want them to get away with it. I was good and mad about it. He was a decent man who had served his country well. It wasn't his fault he was in the state he was in, and he didn't deserve what he got.'

Jake gnawed at his lip. This made no sense to him.

'Why were they so worried?'

'I'd told them I wasn't just going to let it go.'

Jake shook his head. 'I don't mean that. Why did they take him out in the first place?'

'Don't ask me.'

'You don't know?'

Cedric shrugged. 'There must have been some beans they didn't want spilling.'

'But you don't know what they were?'

Cedric sighed. 'It made no sense to me. The man had been out of it for years. What could he know?'

Jake had no idea. He hadn't a clue. And he believed Cedric was telling the truth.

'So they took Caitlin to keep you quiet about Sanderson's death?'

'Yes.'

'For how long?'

'Until the Royal visit's over, they said.'

'What about me?'

'You, Jake?'

'Why try to hit me, as well as Sanderson? What's Donaldson's game?'

Cedric replaced his glasses and stared at Jake. He seemed baffled. 'You mean you don't know?'

'For crissake, Cedric! Know what?'

'Forget about Donaldson, Jake. It's Will Rogers who's running this thing.'

Jake stared for a moment, speechless.

'And don't ask me again what it's about, Jake. I'm not in the loop. They just use people like me when and as they feel like it.'

Jake sat tight. The thoughts buzzed around his head. Rogers? Christ! That made it personal. For him, and for Dixie.

CHAPTER THIRTY-SIX

Bob Cunningham didn't say much.

'Is this line secure?' Jake asked.

'As much as anything can be. It's a mobile.'

'I know it's a mobile. Is it secure?'

'It's my personal phone.'

Jake considered, but not for long. Even if GCHQ's computers were busy monitoring the ether for calls to Bob Cunningham's personal mobile, it would take time for anything to be done about this one.

'You should check out a farmhouse up past Wooler.'

'Go on.'

'A mile or so out of Kirknewton.'

He gave the name of the farm and the grid reference.

'Do you want to tell me why I should check it?' Cunningham asked.

Jake could see him, sitting there at his desk, calm and solid.

'Unless someone else has already got there first, you'll need body bags.'

'How many?'

'Four should be enough.'

The silence was eloquent.

'It's their base,' Jake added. 'Or it was. Remember?'

'I remember. I take it you're not going to make yourself available for questioning?'

'Not yet. But I will do when I get time – if they don't take me out first.'

'Isn't that a tiny bit paranoid?'

'Probably. But I just keep thinking about Sanderson. Are you going to do anything about it now?'

'It's difficult,' Cunningham said heavily.

'Not for me, it isn't. It's straightforward.'

Dixie looked at him after he'd rung off.

'I don't know,' he said in answer to her questioning glance. 'Maybe yes, probably no. Not in time anyway.'

'So it's still down to us?'

He nodded. 'It looks like it.'

'Would we want it any other way, Jake?'

He shook his head and gave her a grim smile. 'I don't think so. Not now. How about you?'

Dixie shook her head slowly. 'Will Rogers,' she said quietly. Then she looked at Jake and added, 'I thought the day would never come.'

CHAPTER THIRTY-SEVEN

'I've known you a long time, Bob.'

'Yes, sir. Best part of thirty years.'

'We've done a lot of good work together.'

'Kind of you to say so, sir.'

The other man scowled, gave him a suspicious look and added, 'And now this.'

'Yes, sir.'

The owner of the office got up from behind his desk, a desk as big as a tennis court, with absolutely nothing on it. It exemplified the clean-desk policy which was supposed to operate at all levels. But it didn't, or at least only on the desks of those with nothing complicated to do, and those who were very efficient.

'Sit over here, Bob,' he suggested, waving Cunningham towards a couple of easy chairs arranged around a chrome and glass coffee table.

Cunningham moved reluctantly. He hated lengthy discussions about the politics of his work. He could see where they were heading.

'Coffee, Bob?'

He was about to say no, no thank-you, but he changed his mind. He knew from experience that sometimes you could only make haste slowly. There were things to consider, a hell of a lot, in fact. Personally, he wouldn't bother. He would just go ahead and do it, whatever it was. That was his way. He couldn't be bothered with the politics. That was one reason why he'd not made Chief Constable. One reason. It was also why he wouldn't have wanted the job even if it had been on offer.

'You've been up there?'

Cunningham nodded. 'Got back half an hour ago.'

'What did you find?'

'Not much. Next to nothing, in fact.'

'But?'

'Forensics will find plenty. My guess is what he told me was spot-on.'

'Four bodies?'

Cunningham nodded.

'Jesus Christ!'

'There's a broken window and some staining that will undoubtedly prove to be blood. There are signs that a lot of people were in the building until very recently.'

'That all?'

'Forensics will find more, a lot more.'

'If we let them loose.'

Cunningham nodded.

They broke off at a knock on the door. The door opened. A middle-aged woman bearing a tray appeared.

'Thanks, Mary,' the Chief Constable murmured as she put the tray down on the little table.

'Will there be anything else, sir?'

He shook his head. 'Field all calls, Mary. I don't want to be disturbed.'

'Are you in court, sir? Or at the dentist's?'

He looked at her and smiled. 'Probably,' he said.

Mary nodded gravely and withdrew.

Cunningham reached for the coffee pot and poured two cups. One he poured black. To his own he added cream and two sugars.

'It'll kill you, that stuff,' the Chief Constable said.

'Coffee?'

'Sugar. And cream.'

'As long as it waits till I've got a bit out of the pension fund.'

'You and me both, Bob. We deserve that.' He paused and added, 'I suppose we should inform our . . . our colleagues from London.'

Both MI5 and the Met, he meant.

Cunningham nodded. 'Like they inform us about everything, sir. Absolutely everything.'

He waited, while trying not to appear as if he was waiting. It was in the balance now. Go through the proper channels. Do things the bureaucrats' way. Or . . . Or not.

'It's on our patch, Bob.'

'Yes, sir.'

'And on my watch! Four bodies?'

'Plus the others I'm told have been disappeared.'

'You believe him?'

Cunningham nodded. 'I do. He may be in it up to his neck, but it's in his own interest to get us on side. That's why he's come to me.'

'But to what end? What's going on?'

'We might never know, sir – not altogether. I think we should just keep it simple. Crimes have been committed. More are probably intended. We need to police the situation. That would be my advice – if you were to ask, sir.'

'Our friends are not telling us much, are they?'

MI5 and the Met, again, thought Cunningham as he shook his head.

'A Royal assassination on our watch? While we twiddle our thumbs? Unthinkable!'

'Yes, sir.'

'Right. Get Forensics up to the farmhouse. See if you can get anything more out of your informant. I'll have Charlie Mavin flood the streets with his uniforms tomorrow. We'll come up with some cock-and-bull story to deal with any complaints from our friends from the south. And I'll speak to the Chairman of the Committee. Square the politicians. Ours, at least – the ones that matter to us. That do you, Bob?'

Bob Cunningham grinned. 'Perfectly, sir!'

CHAPTER THIRTY-EIGHT

Jake got them all together – all except Caitlin. It was the middle of the night, and they were tired, but they had to make things happen. They could sleep the rest of their lives.

'I want to pool our knowledge,' he said, 'and try to make sense of what's happening here before it's too late. We're almost out of time.'

He looked round at them. Dixie was calm and looked poised for action, even if she was tired. He was sure she would rather be outside, but this was where she was right now. She had no complaints. She was OK.

Anna was holding together, as well. She looked exhausted, but she was game. He judged her fatigue was probably more psychological than physical; she wasn't used to being stressed like this. She was too young and inexperienced. He would have liked her to stay young and inexperienced, too, he thought fondly, but it was too late for that.

Cedric was visibly distracted. Agitated, but resigned. He would rather be somewhere else. His body language said he'd done his bit, and this wasn't his fight. But it was. Too damn right, it was! Jake thought bleakly. You're not getting out of this, old friend. If you'd levelled with me in the beginning, we might not be where we are now.

'I should be with Caitlin,' Cedric said anxiously.

'Stay where you are.'

'You have no right. . . .'

'Shut up and sit down! If you'd said something a long time ago, things might be different now. You stay here. Caitlin's fine.'

Cedric looked ready to argue for a moment, then he subsided. The chair creaked beneath his weight as he settled more firmly into it. 'You're right, Jake,' he admitted. 'I should have told you things.'

'But you didn't. Now shut up! We haven't time.'

Anna glanced at him, surprised by the exchange. He winked at her. He wanted her to know it was a performance.

Dixie looked indifferent. Dixie wasn't a people person.

'Let's see what we know,' Jake began. 'And let's see if we can work out what the game plan is here. Let's brainstorm, if you like. What's happening, and why.'

'Publicity?' Anna suggested, kicking it off.

'For what?'

'Some cause? Some belief?'

'What, though?' Jake asked. 'Anti-monarchy? The Middle East? Anti-UK? Anti-Western?'

'And why?' Dixie followed up. 'Why are they doing it here and now?'

This point stifled the burgeoning discussion. The suggestions died. They couldn't link the possible causes to the people they knew to be involved. It was hard even to get started.

'We seem to have a rogue element in the Security Service,' Jake suggested. 'Donaldson appears to be at the centre of it. What's he after? And what about Will Rogers? Cedric thinks he's behind it. How does he fit in?'

He glanced at Anna, who shrugged. 'I've never heard of a Will Rogers. Not that that means anything. What do I know?'

'Focus on Donaldson for the moment,' Dixie suggested. 'He's the guy who's driving it on the ground. What's he like?'

Jake nodded. 'What do we know about him, Anna?'

'He's intelligent, articulate, experienced, in a senior position, ambitious . . .' Anna broke off and shrugged. 'An important member of the Department. Highly competent and going places, I'm told.'

'What's he for?' Jake said. 'What's his purpose?'

'Security. Security of the Realm.'

Jake smiled. Oh, yes! he thought. That helps.

'OK. Security. That's what he's there for. To protect the nation, and members of the nation. To protect the State, and the organs of the State.

Officially, that's what he's for. Anything else?'

'Money?' Dixie said. 'That often plays a part. It's a great motivator.'

'Money – Donaldson?' Jake looked at her. 'Maybe. But where's the money in this thing? Assuming he wants money, where could it be coming from? Oil dollars? Fundamentalists?'

'They have plenty of it,' Dixie pointed out. 'Cash is one thing they're not short of in the Middle East. Other places, as well. Even in Afghanistan and Somalia they seem to be able to come up with it when they need it.'

'They're not short of belief either,' Anna pointed out. 'Another motivating force.'

There was silence for a moment. They each tried to think more coherent thoughts. This is hopeless! Jake thought. We're not getting very far.

'You're heading into a blind alley,' Cedric said slowly, ponderously, coming awake, joining in at last. 'Don't go down there.'

'No, hang on, Ced!' Jake said. 'Let's throw it around a bit more.'

'No, Jake. You're wrong. He's not motivated by money.'

'Do you know that for a fact? Do you know him?'

Cedric nodded.

'Well, what is he motivated by?'

'Ideas, commitment. If he's anything, he's a devout nationalist. If you like, a fundamentalist.'

Jake stared at him a moment. 'Go on,' he said quietly. 'What else do you know?'

'Not much, to be honest, but there are one or two things you should be aware of.'

'We're listening,' Dixie said pointedly.

'I believe, as Anna says, he is committed to the job,' Cedric said slowly. 'Committed to the job, that is, as he sees it.'

'Of course he is,' Anna said. 'He wouldn't have got where he is if he wasn't.'

'Ced?' Jake said calmly. 'What else do you know?'

Cedric adjusted his glasses before he spoke again. 'He's not English-born. I know that.'

'What do you mean?'

'He's foreign, by birth.'

'Come on!'

'It's true.'

'How do you know that?'

Cedric shrugged. 'I know. That's all.'

'Even if you're right, what difference does it make? Plenty of people in high places were born in other countries, colonies or whatever. If not them, their parents were.'

'You'd have a hard time in the US, taking that line,' Dixie said. 'Foreign-born? Who isn't!'

Cedric shook his head stubbornly. 'If there's one truly important thing about him,' he said, 'it's that.'

'Humour me, Cedric,' Jake said softly. 'I'm not on your wavelength yet.'

'He's more English, more British rather, than most people born in these islands. He chose to be here, and to throw in his lot with us. And he works to keep the country as he thinks it should be. That's all I'm saying. Somehow that underlies whatever is happening here.'

'Assassinating the heir to the throne?' Anna said sarcastically.

Cedric nodded. 'Even that,' he said, 'if he believes it's necessary.'

Jake thought about it for a moment. Cedric had put a different slant on things. He wondered if it was worth thinking about. It might explain the rogue element in the Security Service. He felt a need to mull it over.

'Let's break for five minutes,' he suggested.

He walked over to the far end of the room, away from the others, and stared at the blank screen of a small TV without seeing it. Donaldson as arch nationalist? If you fed that into the broth, what did it taste like? How did it help? How could assassinating the Prince of Wales help?

He couldn't see it. He couldn't see how that would help anybody.

Without conscious thought, just fiddling really, he leaned forward and switched on the TV. As the picture appeared, he saw a small group of official looking people with a woman in the middle approaching a big building. They went through fancy glass doors. It looked like Edinburgh, the Scottish Parliament building. Probably part of a late news programme.

He switched channels. For another few moments he watched some football team in white shirts playing a team in blue shirts. The ones in white shirts seemed upset about something the man in black had done, or had not done.

He switched channels again and studied a weather map. Wet, wet, wet, but less wet in the east. He went back to the delegation visiting the building that looked like the Scottish Parliament for a moment. Then he switched the TV off.

'Quite a weekend for them,' Dixie said over his shoulder. 'All this travelling.'

'Who?'

'Wasn't that his sister?'

'Whose sister?'

'The heir to the throne's sister!'

He realized he hadn't consciously registered who the woman was in the little party entering the building. Dixie was right, though. He glanced back at the screen. It was blank now.

'So?'

'Nothing. Small talk.'

Jake continued staring at the screen for a few moments, even though it remained blank. Then he shook his head and walked slowly back to join the others. His head was suddenly buzzing.

'OK, everybody,' he said. 'Let's start again.

'Jake?' Anna said, concern in her voice. 'Are you all right?'

He shook his head and flashed a smile. 'Just thinking,' he said.

Anna smiled back. 'Does it hurt that badly?'

'Sometimes it does, yes.'

He turned to Cedric. 'The Prince is here, probably staying in Alnwick. The Princess Royal there, in Edinburgh, eighty-odd miles away. They seem to be gathering in force in this part of the country. Any significance in that that you can see?'

Cedric pushed his glasses more firmly onto his nose and squinted myopically. 'Significance? You mean is something else going on?'

'I don't know. Just wondering. What do you think? Will they meet up somewhere, or just go their separate ways?'

'Hard to say. They do like Scotland, though. They all spend a lot of time there, the Royals, don't they?'

'The PM is Scottish, isn't he?' Anna offered.

'Like a lot of the Labour MPs,' Jake said. 'So?'

'I don't know. I'm just brainstorming, as you said.'

Jake nodded. 'Good. Keep it up. Anything else, anyone?'

'He might be coming here,' Anna reminded him.

Jake stared. Of course. He'd forgotten that.

'Who might?' Dixie asked.

'The Prime Minister,' Jake said. 'Anything in that, Cedric?'

'The PM coming here?'

'Yes. Maybe.'

'Probably, actually,' Anna said, 'though it's not certain. It all depends . . . what?' she said, looking impatiently at Jake.

'You didn't say "probably" when you first mentioned it.'

'Well, excuse me! *Probably* he is. That better?'

'Our friend Donaldson won't like it,' Cedric said.

Jake looked at him.

'He's not fond of the Scots. Not the hairy ones, at least. The real Scots.'

'For crissake, Ced!' Jake said, becoming irritated.

Cedric shrugged. 'He's always going on about the Scot Nats, and their ilk.'

'I don't understand,' Dixie said, looking perplexed.

'Some Scots want independence from England,' Jake said.

'Really? After all this time?'

'Let's not get into that now.'

'He particularly doesn't like MacGregor,' Cedric added.

'The Prime Minister?' Jake said. 'Why the hell not?'

'Thinks he's too soft on them, the Scot Nats, that is. He's from Berwick, this is his constituency. Thinks they ought to be crushed before they get out of hand. To him, MacGregor is a weak and vacillating character who doesn't know how to handle them. Donaldson thinks he's a sympathiser, even.'

'That's democracy for you,' Dixie said.

'Oh, he doesn't like that either,' Cedric said. 'Not really. He likes the kind they have in countries like Pakistan and Belarus, the kind you can switch on and off when it suits you. If you don't like the election result, the President ignores it or the Army takes over. Both, sometimes.'

'Where?' Anna said.

Cedric looked at her. 'Where what?'

'Where did you say? I heard Pakistan. But what was the other place you mentioned?'

'Come on!' Jake said. 'We haven't got time for this.'

'Belarus,' Cedric said. 'Where he came from.'

There was a stunned silence.

'Say that again,' Jake said, astonished.

'Which part?'

'Where did you say he's from?' Anna asked.

'Belarus.'

'You guys!' Dixie said. 'I can't believe I'm hearing this.' She looked at Jake, a hopeless expression on her face. 'Is your friend for real?'

Jake felt things were slipping away from him. Doors were opening he hadn't even suspected might be there. It was like being in a space probe that was disintegrating.

'Donaldson, you're talking about?' he queried.

Cedric nodded. 'Or Rogers. Whatever you prefer to call him.'

'Stop it, Ced! We haven't got time to fuck around like this.'

Jake was angry now. The whole thing was falling apart. People fooling around. It was becoming a party game.

'He means it, Jake,' Dixie said equably.

'Means what?'

He glanced from Dixie to Cedric, and back again.

'He means it,' Dixie repeated.

Jake slowed down. Stopped. He turned and stared at Cedric. 'You meant that?'

Cedric nodded.

'Jesus Christ!'

Jake sat down, feeling unutterably weary. 'You sure about this, Ced?' he asked after a moment. 'Or are you just pissing me about?'

'Reasonably sure.'

'How can you know all this?' Anna demanded. 'I never knew he was from . . . wherever you said.'

Cedric looked at Jake, who nodded to him to continue.

'I once spent time with Donaldson – or Rogers, as some of us know him better as – in a place, a situation, from which we didn't expect to emerge alive. Neither of us did. But we had time to kill, if you'll excuse the pun. We spoke of many things in what we thought was the time we had left.'

'But you survived?' Anna said. 'Obviously.'

'Obviously,' Cedric agreed.

'Is that why he stayed in contact with you afterwards?' Jake asked.

'Possibly. I've often wondered. At first I used to be surprised he didn't just have me eliminated. Then I realized I was useful to him from time to time. I don't know, maybe I was just flattering myself. Probably the real reason was I wasn't important enough, or he couldn't find the time.'

'No,' Jake said, shaking his head. 'That wasn't it. He wanted you to watch out for Sanderson – and me, as well. You were useful.'

'Whatever,' Cedric said. He closed his eyes, as if worn out by all the talking.

'You came to Cragley after me, didn't you? He sent you. And then Sanderson.'

Cedric nodded.

'And I thought you were a friend!' Jake said bitterly.

'You have become one, Jake,' Cedric said plaintively. 'Truly.'

Jake snorted and turned away. 'Anna,' he said, 'when those guys tried to abduct you, did they at any time speak in a language other than English? Or did they have a foreign accent?'

'No. They spoke normal English.'

'One of them spoke Russian,' Dixie said quietly. 'When I was checking his pulse. He muttered a bit in Russian before he died.'

'Russian? How would you know that?' Anna asked. 'Oh, of course!' she added with a sniff, as Dixie gave her a cool look. 'You would, would-n't you?'

Dixie didn't respond.

Jake could see there was no doubt in Dixie's mind about what she had heard. And he accepted that. Dixie did many things well, including speaking Russian.

'Ced?' he said. 'That would be right, would it? The language?'

'For a Belarussian? Yes, of course.'

Jake nodded. 'So now we know where his henchmen came from,' he said bitterly to Anna. 'Belarus, for crissake!'

'I'm not even sure where it is,' Anna said plaintively.

'Next to Poland and Ukraine,' Dixie said crisply. 'And Russia, of course. It's the one part of the former Soviet Union that's not changed its nature. A sort of Stalinist democracy, if that's not an oxymoron.'

'Oxymoron?' Anna said. 'Is that American English?'

'Stop it!' Jake said.

Anna shrugged.

'So what have we got here?' Jake added with a sigh, wondering how to pull everything back together again.

'Enough, maybe?' Cedric said.

Jake gave him a brief smile. 'Oh, yes,' he said. 'I'm sure we have. I think we can guess now why he wanted Sanderson and me out of the way.'

He looked across at Dixie, who nodded. She knew, too.

'Why?' Anna asked, looking puzzled and clearly feeling out of it.

'We would recognise him,' he told her. 'We know Ed Donaldson is Will Rogers.'

'So?'

'Tell her, Cedric.'

'He took another man's identity,' Cedric said tersely. 'When we escaped, and survived, he became Ed Donaldson.'

'And you let him?' Anna said incredulously.

Cedric looked uncomfortable. 'I was afraid of him,' he said. 'Afraid of what he was capable of doing to Caitlin and me.'

There was a moment's silence for reflection. Then Jake said, 'You're on borrowed time, Ced.'

Cedric nodded. 'Have been for years.'

'You were useful for a time,' Jake added gently, 'but now you're unfinished business.'

Cedric nodded again.

'Take Caitlin and move out. Go somewhere safe.'

Cedric shook his head.

'At least until this thing is over,' Jake persisted. 'If it works out well, come back. If it doesn't ....'

'We're staying,' Cedric said flatly. He took off his glasses and gazed at Jake in a kindly way. 'Thank you for your concern, Jake, but we're staying. We've had enough of running scared.'

'I hoped you might say that,' Jake said softly.

CHAPTER THIRTY-NINE

'I'd better see how Caitlin is,' Cedric said.

'Yes,' Jake said. 'You go, Ced.'

'Sure?'

'We can manage now.'

Cedric levered himself up and shuffled towards the door. Anna put the kettle on to make more coffee.

'It's a morass,' Dixie said. 'We're getting deeper and deeper.'

'Isn't it?' Jake said equably.

He felt better somehow. Complexities, yes, but at last things were beginning to make some sort of sense.

'Coffee, Dixie?' Anna called.

'Please.'

Jake looked at Dixie with surprise.

'I feel the need for more energy,' she explained, 'after hearing all that.'

He smiled and nodded, and waited for the coffee.

Rogers, eh? Or Donaldson. He wondered how he chose what name to use, and what his real name, his original name, was. He wondered if anyone knew. Even him any more.

He also wondered how he'd got into this situation in the first place. Well, maybe it hadn't been that difficult. A lot of people had changed their colours after the Berlin Wall had come down. And then, later, effective service with the Secret Service could well have been regarded as good qualification for the Security Service. Especially when they were so desperate for Arabic speakers.

He shook his head. So easy! It didn't bear thinking about.

'What are we going to do?' Anna asked as she brought over a steaming mug for him.

'Two things,' Jake said. 'First, we need to find the sniper's nest, and take him out. Second we need to bring Donaldson down, and. . . .'

'Bring him to justice,' Anna completed.

'Take him out,' Dixie corrected her.

Anna stared at her and then at Jake. 'Bring him to justice,' she repeated, this time with a small question mark.

'Take him out,' Jake said firmly. 'It's personal,' he added for Anna's benefit. 'He's crossed the line. And for us, it's personal.'

Anna just stared.

'How many men has he got left, do you think?' Jake asked Dixie.

'Not many.' Dixie shrugged. 'We know about the two who left the farmhouse early, and we know there's a sniper. Not many more. Not here, at least.'

'If any,' Anna said.

'If any,' Jake agreed.

'He only needs the sniper, anyway,' Dixie pointed out. 'He doesn't really need anybody else. Not now.'

'OK. Dixie, you keep on looking for the sniper. Anna, work the phones. Find out anything you can about the visit. Updated arrangements. Find out if they know yet if the PM is actually coming.

'I'll be on the street,' he added. 'And around and about.'

He glanced at his watch. 'Five o'clock now. Dark for another hour or so. Then it's going to be busy. Let's go!'

The light came flooding into Main Street, and with it the start of a new day. Amazingly, there were still milkmen in this part of the world. Jake watched one of them placing bottles on silent door steps. Mist from the North Sea had come upriver with the tide. Now it swirled around the man, blurring his outline, making it shiver. The clink and chink of bottles marked his passage as he receded into the mist.

'Anything?'

He glanced over his shoulder at Anna and shook his head.

'You should get some rest, Jake.'

She was right, but he knew he wouldn't sleep, not now it was daylight. The others could do that, but not him.

'I'm OK. Besides, we haven't got the time. It's the day after tomorrow, remember?'

'Wrong. It's tomorrow now, Jake. This is Thursday.'

Shit! So it was. He grimaced. He must be tired.

Anna came and peered over his shoulder. She shivered. 'Not much of a day, is it?'

'I'm happy just to see it.'

She nodded. She knew, as well as he did, that last night might have ended differently. As for today . . . he had no idea what to expect.

'How's Caitlin?'

'Asleep. Recovering, hopefully.'

He nodded. 'Dixie?'

'No idea. Out somewhere.'

He didn't ask about Cedric. He would find that out for himself.

'Maybe I will lie down for a bit,' he said. 'Try to get some rest.'

'I'll wake you if anything happens.'

'You'd better!'

She grinned and kissed his cheek. He reached for her and hugged her hard, closing his eyes, breathing in the scent of her, feeling the warmth of her, relishing the arms wrapped around him. When he relaxed his grip, she released him reluctantly. He smoothed her face with the palm of his hand and moved away from the window.

Bed, and sleep, suddenly seemed a good idea. It was as if some of the tension had left him with the arrival of daylight. Maybe it would be possible to grab a couple of hours sleep after all.

He lay down. The bed was warm still from Anna. He could feel the pattern of her body in the heat contours of the mattress and the quilt. He re-lived the sense of abandon he had found with her a few hours earlier. They had been good together. They could be again. They just needed more time.

Time. There it was again. Time, the great thief. Who was it said that? Somebody. Somebody important, or well known. But he couldn't remember who. Typical!

Only today left. Then tomorrow. Tomorrow was pressing heavily.

He dozed fitfully for a little while but real sleep wouldn't come. Not now, however tired he was. He abandoned the quest and levered himself out of bed.

Anna looked round at him with mock disapproval. 'Speed sleeping?' she asked with a grin. 'Five minutes enough?'

He forced a smile. 'Something came up. My brain's too busy. Do you know what the programme is for tomorrow?'

'Of course.'

He gave a wry smile. 'That's good. I assumed you were. . . .'

'What? Outside the loop? Just walking the streets?'

'Well . . .' His smile became a grin. 'Something like that. Talk me through it.'

'It starts early. The Prince arrives at 2pm, but the programme begins at 7am. Or even 6.' She frowned as she tried to remember. 'Six, I think.'

'What happens then?'

'Things start. In fact, they start this afternoon. The police will be out putting up no-parking signs and warning notices on cars parked near the building.

'Then, tomorrow morning, they start at six. Tow-trucks are brought in to remove any vehicles from the clear zone. Tapes and removable barriers are put up. Traffic cones. All that.'

'How big is the zone?'

'I'm not sure. A hundred yards on Main Street. Maybe more.'

'And the side streets?'

'Of course.' She thought again. 'And they'll close off the bottom end of Main Street and establish a detour for the day.'

Standard practice. Routine. Much as he would have expected. The roads near the building would be cleared, and kept clear.

None of this would worry a sniper, of course. In fact, it would make his job easier. Less clutter. Less movement. Better focus.

'So that's the police accounted for. Unless they're going to do anything else?' he suggested.

She shook her head. 'I don't think so. Just keep the roads clear and control the crowds. That sort of thing.'

'Right. Who else will be there?'

'Our people are supposed to keep an eye on things from a distance. Or they were supposed to.' She frowned. 'I don't know now.'

'We'll come back to that.'

'Then the Royal Protection squad will be in close attendance. Bodyguards. Protocol.'

'The local Special Branch?'

'I don't know now.' She broke off, despairing. 'I just don't know!'

'Cup of coffee?' he asked, to break the building tension.

She nodded. He got up and started making it. She got up from the chair and took up position beside the window again. She seemed unnerved by the gaps in her knowledge, and perhaps by the realization of what might happen very soon if they couldn't stop it. Big responsibility. She hadn't bargained on this when she left London.

'They're coming in by helicopter?' he asked, knowing the answer but needing to get her talking again.

She nodded. 'Most of them are.'

'Most of them?'

'The PM isn't. He's coming direct from his constituency by car – if he can make it.'

'Why is he coming anyway?'

'He pretty well has to, doesn't he? It's his constituency.' She shrugged. 'It's a courtesy matter. Protocol. You can't visit an MP's backyard without inviting him along. But it was pretty late in the day when we were given his schedule. We now know he's coming – unless he gets detained, of course.'

Jake shook his head. Jesus! The Prime Minister as well. 'Makes it an even bigger target,' he said.

'I suppose so.'

'It doesn't make much difference in a practical sense, though,' Jake said slowly. 'The Prince arrives by chopper. He lands in the fields alongside the river and a car takes him to the housing project, where he possibly meets the PM.'

He frowned. 'That's when they'll do it. Outside, as they gather on the steps for photos. Just before they go in. That's when I'd do it – stationary target – maximum publicity.'

'Is that what they want? Publicity?'

'I would think so. That's likely to be the whole point. Maximum publicity, maximum damage.'

'Damage to what, though?' she said quietly. 'What's Ed's game?'

'Wish I knew,' he said with a shrug.

CHAPTER FORTY

It came down to just two buildings in the end. Just the two that from the outside, at least, offered the best prospects for a sniper.

One, Mains House, was the building next to the Narrow Nick that had the florist's at ground-floor level. The other, Netherton Place, was right next to the guest house from which she had extricated Anna. From the upper floors of both there was a clear line of sight on the front entrance to the housing project. And both had discreet rear exits.

Mains House had three floors above ground level. Dixie studied the name plates at the entrance before she went inside. The first floor was occupied by 'The Johnsons'; the second by 'A.E. Hodges', and the third by 'Jack Cummings'.

She could hear nothing on the two upper floors. Behind 'The Johnsons' door on the first floor she could hear a television and lots of small-children noises. A family, then, she decided. She could rule that one out. She would come back to the upper flats.

Netherton Place was different. There were offices on the first two floors, one an accountant's, the other occupied by some sort of insurance broker. Flat One and Flat Two, on the second floor, she guessed were holiday flats; they were both empty now. The top floor had only one flat, with the name 'G. Roberts' hand-written on a faded card on the door. That, too, was empty.

They were no good, though. Any of them. As soon as she got inside she realized that. The windows were too big and too front-on. It would be impossible for a sniper to set up without being visible from outside. The same applied to the offices.

Mains House was much better. Ideal, in fact. It was a little further away, and it was set slightly back and at more of an angle. The windows were smaller, too. Small panes of glass. When open they would be a lot less conspicuous than any of the windows in Netherton Place.

It would be the flat on the second floor or the one on the third floor, she decided. Windows at both levels were open already, presumably to offset the heat build-up in south-facing rooms. So people would be used to seeing them open. That would be a help.

The flat occupied by A.E. Hodges on the second floor would be her own preference. One floor less to descend when making your escape.

She returned to Mains House and mounted the stairs, hearing again the sound of children in the first-floor flat as she passed. Her knock on A.E. Hodges's door produced a disappointing response. The door swung open to reveal a balding, middle-aged man wearing strangely coloured glasses. He peered at her.

'Mr Cummings?' she said.

'No.'

'Oh?'

The man stared at her suspiciously and then said, 'Upstairs. He has the upstairs flat.'

'Oh?' she said again. 'Have I got it wrong? I thought . . . never mind! Sorry to bother you.'

'Not at all.'

He didn't respond, but he watched suspiciously as she began her ascent to the next floor. She hoped Jack Cummings wasn't in. Otherwise she was going to have some explaining to do.

'He is not there!' A.E. Hodges suddenly called after her.

'No?' she said, half-turning.

'He is not back from his work.'

She turned to face him. 'Where does he work?'

The man shook his head. 'I only know he is not here. I hear him,' he added, 'when he is home, but I haven't heard anything today.'

Dixie descended the stairs. 'Thank you,' she said, continuing on her way. 'I'll come back later.'

She felt him watching her descend the stairs and knew she needed to be careful if she was not to heighten his suspicions. Already he would have realized she was American, but that couldn't be helped. She was what she was. Anyway, he had a funny accent himself. He couldn't criticize her.

At least she knew now where the sniper would be located. The top-floor flat was empty all day. So that's where he would be. The unfortunate Jack Cummings wouldn't even know anyone had ever been there. Not until the cops arrested him.

Next morning she could hear the children downstairs again. Their laughter and squeals of excitement, banter and protests were clearly audible. They were getting ready for a day off school; a big day for them, and for Cragley. Maybe for the entire country, though few knew that yet.

She didn't mind the noise. The sounds the children made were happy, comfortable sounds. A person living here would miss them if they were absent.

There was still no sign of Jack Cummings. She had been in position early but had seen and heard no-one go to work from his flat. No-one else had come either. Time was moving on, and she was getting tired of this broom cupboard.

At ten she moved out. She emerged cautiously from the cupboard, slipped across the landing, fiddled with the lock and opened the door to the flat. There was no-one inside. And it didn't look as if anyone had been there for some time. No dirty crockery stacked in the sink. The rubbish bin was empty and clean. There was a small jumble of mail scattered on the door mat, some bills, bank statements and circulars – nothing out of the ordinary.

She looked further. The flat was a home, not a holiday flat. There were clothes in the wardrobe and in the chest of drawers in the bedroom. She opened the fridge door and wrinkled her nose. There were plenty of bottles and jars, a packet of cheese; some eggs and three bottles of beer. The bad smell was from milk that had gone off. She picked up the carton and shook it. Not so much milk any more as cheese. It had been rancid for some time.

Jack Cummings was a young guy. His stuff said that. Jeans and T-shirts in the wardrobe. Posters of bands she had never heard of on the walls. So maybe he had a girlfriend with a place of her own? Or he'd gone on holiday? Something, anyway. He certainly wasn't here now.

Then again, maybe he wasn't coming back – ever? She grimaced. Maybe someone had wanted this room really badly. She hoped not.

If that was the case, they would need to be here soon. They were running out of time.

She kept back from the window, but could see that preparations in the village were well underway. As Anna had forecast, the police had cordoned off the street. Parked cars had been removed, one way or another, and bollards were being put in place. Temporary fencing to keep the anticipated crowds in place was visible. Things were happening.

She settled herself in a corner of the room to wait. Whoever came through the door, she would see them before they saw her. She laid her gun beside her.

By 10.30, she began to worry she had made a mistake. Maybe she was in the wrong place, after all? Time was ebbing fast.

At 11, she wondered why the man downstairs had said he hadn't heard Jack Cummings return home from work the previous day. Judging by the milk in the refrigerator, he couldn't have heard him do that for some time – days, maybe even a week or two.

She shook her head. People! Especially those living alone. They lost track. Didn't know one week from another, half of them.

The window was open. She heard vehicles moving through the village. She heard people milling about on the pavements below. The sun moved behind cloud, and back out again. A fresh breeze stirred the trees on the green. She began to fret.

Her phone vibrated. She glanced at it and answered cautiously.

'Anything?' Jake enquired.

'Nothing.'

'Same here.'

'Jake, I'm worried.'

'Plenty of time.'

'Ask Anna what the police said about this building when they came round.'

'I'll get back to you.'

She hoped she'd got it right. If she hadn't, she was in the wrong place.

Her phone vibrated again.

'Mains House?' Anna said.

'Yeah.'

'They said . . . let me see.' She consulted her notes. 'They said: florist on ground floor, Johnson family on first. Second and third floors both vacant.'

That was odd.

'Oh, wait a moment!' Anna said. 'That's wrong. Occupant of top floor flat on holiday for two weeks. Just the other one empty.'

She thought for a moment. Empty? It didn't make sense. Unless. . . .

'The flat on the second floor is vacant?'

'That's right.'

'Except it isn't.'

'It's supposed to be.' There was a pause. Then: 'Do you think. . . ?'

'Thanks, Anna.'

She ended the call.

So what about A.E. Hodges?

She let herself out of the flat and quietly descended the stairs. On the floor below she studied the name card. There it was: 'A.E. Hodges'. Very visible and very clear. Impossible to miss or mistake.

But the card was obviously new, now she looked closely at it. The police hadn't missed it, or got it wrong. It simply hadn't been there when they came round.

She hesitated. A new tenant? So soon? He'd not looked new. And this seemed to be a building for young people, or people between things. Not well settled, middle-aged men who looked as if they wore slippers and old-fashioned pyjamas half the day. Strange.

She put her ear to the door and kept it there until she heard someone clearing their throat. He was home. Someone was.

She hesitated a moment longer. She might have got it wrong, in which case she would have some explaining to do. On the other hand. . . .

It was worth the risk.

She eyed the door a moment and then raised her foot and stamped hard on the lock. The door gave way and crashed open.

Immediately she saw different things, all in slow motion. She saw A.E. Hodges turn round with surprise, peering at her from behind those unusual glasses he wore, which she realized now were probably to focus the light. She saw the mounting on the table in the middle of the room, the mounting holding the rifle and the scope and the bits and pieces that were all part of the tool bag of the sniper. She saw A.E. Hodges lifting a hand gun from the table and swinging round to point it at her.

She was off-balance from the manoeuvre required to kick the door in, and was falling forward into the room. A.E. Hodges was ahead of her. He was surprisingly fast. His hand gun was almost in line with her. He couldn't miss from this distance.

She let herself tumble forward, making no attempt to arrest her momentum. Instead she used it to hurtle across the floor. She fired from the prone position while the hand gun was still tracking her movements. She managed to fire twice before in her tumbling momentum she lost sight of A.E. Hodges.

When she came up hard against the wall, she pushed off desperately with feet and one arm. She swung round, lifting her gun arm, to see A.E.Hodges falling fast. The hand gun had left his grip and was floating through the air towards her. She hadn't heard its bark. She hadn't felt anything. And she knew she'd hit him. He was going down.

She pushed herself upright, ready to fire again. There was no need. Even before she reached him, she could see the last of the life ebb out of him.

She closed the door and drew breath. Then she pulled out her phone and used it.

'Got him!' she said.

CHAPTER FORTY-ONE

Jake told Dixie that she'd done well, and to get the hell out of there. Then he rang Bob Cunningham.

'The sniper was in Mains House, Bob. Second floor. Supposedly occupied by an A.E. Hodges.'

'Is he alive?'

'No.'

'Nothing to do with you, I suppose?'

'Not really. I'd be happy to take any kind of test you care to arrange to establish that I haven't fired a weapon in the recent past.'

'You mean today?'

'Today.'

'We might have to come back to that.' Cunningham paused and then said, 'Off the record, Jake, someone's done a fine job there. Are we out of the woods now, do you think?'

'I don't know. I really don't. I'd like to think so but I've got a funny feeling about this. So many loose ends and unanswered questions. It's like there's something we're missing here.'

'Just about everything, it seems to me,' the other man said with a sigh.

Jake couldn't put his finger on it. But there was some reason he didn't feel like celebrating. Maybe it was just that it wasn't a joyous sort of occasion. Or maybe it was because Ed Donaldson, aka Will Rogers, was still around for whatever reason, it didn't feel as though it was over.

'What about Donaldson?' he asked.

'We can't touch him, yet, if ever. We have no reason to.'

That was disappointing, but about right. The police would need more than gut instinct and hearsay to make a move against him. He and Dixie didn't, though, Jake thought grimly. They just needed a chance.

'Donaldson,' Jake said. 'He used to be known as Rogers, Will Rogers.'

'Did he now?'

'When I knew him, that's who he was. But even that's not the name he started off with.'

'Spooks, eh?'

'Spooks.'

'There's been a small change of plan, by the way,' Cunningham added. 'I don't know if it affects anything significantly but the Prime Minister is running late. Something came up. So now we're having to provide a fast escort service to get him here.'

'The Royal visit goes ahead, though?'

'Oh, yes! We recommended postponement but they wouldn't hear of it.'

'The Met or the Security Service?'

'The Prince of Wales. He said it was his duty.'

Jake winced and wondered if the man was as smart as he was brave.

'He would, of course,' Cunningham added, 'being who he is. I have a lot of respect for the man these days. So come hail or come shine, the Willy Morgan Housing Project will be opened officially right on time by His Royal Highness the Prince of Wales, hopefully with the Prime Minister in attendance – if we can get him here. And, from what you tell me, we can all breathe easier about it going ahead now.'

'Not while Donaldson is still in the game, we can't. He won't have given up.'

'No, perhaps not, but things are happening on that front, as well. MI5 and the Met seem to have realized something's gone wrong. Don't ask me how. I don't know.

'But the Chief Constable tells me Donaldson's colleagues are looking for him. And they've put out a warning that he's . . . well, "run amok" is a phrase that seems to cover it. My Chief Constable says he's never heard anything like it.'

'How about you, Bob?'

'Me? I try not to be surprised by anything this job throws at me, but sometimes it's hard going.'

Jake smiled but his heart began to beat a little faster. He wondered what had happened. 'Maybe too many people have been disappearing?' he suggested.

'Maybe. I wouldn't be surprised. You've done your bit though, Jake, you and whoever's been helping you.'

'What did he say?' Anna asked.

'He's grateful, I think. He doesn't know about Dixie, but he realizes someone special is doing things out there. Perhaps he thinks it's you,' he added with a smile and a sly sideways glance.

'Maybe he does. What's funny about that?'

'Nothing! Nothing at all.'

She pretended to be un-placated. 'So what now?'

'I think you should get outside and see if you can spot Donaldson anywhere. Your department is distancing itself from him, apparently. Something's happened.'

'That's interesting.'

'Isn't it?'

'What about you, Jake?'

'I'm going to stay here.'

'Doing what?'

'I'm going to stay here and think.'

'Nice.'

'Get out of here!'

The crowd was building up nicely. Even from where he stood watching, Jake could hear the hum of eager expectation. There were children from the First School, with their teachers and their Union flags; pensioners; people intent on enjoying the spectacle, unaware that it might be a bigger one than they had anticipated.

He watched Anna for a while as she threaded her way through the crowd. When he lost her, he turned his attention to the windows opposite. He wondered if the other side had given up now that they had lost so many men. His uneasy guess, however, was that they hadn't – precisely because they had lost so many men.

And if Donaldson, or Rogers, really was in trouble, that would probably serve to stiffen his resolve. He would go for broke now. He had nothing to lose.

He gave a start and pulled back from the window. For a moment he thought he had seen a once familiar face in the crowd. The years seemed to roll away; anger coursed through his body. If he had exacted revenge for Ellie then, none of this would be happening now. Rogers had prospered because everyone else had respected the rules.

He didn't see the face again. Perhaps he had not seen it at all. He'd just spent too much time thinking about the person that went with the face.

The tension grew as the time drew nearer. He could feel it coming in waves from the street. The buzz. The excited chatter. The low hum of crowds of youngsters waiting in subdued, nervous suspense. The occasional outbursts at false alarms.

It affected him as much as anybody. He wiped his brow with the back of one hand and concentrated. He didn't know what he was looking for, waiting for, but he knew he would recognize it when it came.

He heard the chopper coming in. The sound of it filled the valley and sent swarms of rooks into the sky in alarm. Jake couldn't see it but he felt and heard it, and he visualized it circling the field where it would land. Slow and heavy, ponderous, vulnerable, it would make an ideal target for someone fearless with a RPG. Fearless, or someone who didn't care what happened to himself.

He took the call on his mobile. Dixie said, 'They're down.'

'Anyone close?'

'Negative. The field's empty. Or it was. The police have just waved through three official cars. They're heading for the chopper.'

'Three cars?'

'They look OK. One full of VIPs. One full of suits – Intelligence, or whatever. Some bodyguards, presumably.'

'And the third?'

'Empty.'

It sounded right. Empty car for the Royal visitors.

'Cars moving out,' Dixie said a minute or two later.

It wouldn't be long now. Five minutes max. Jake visualized them trav-elling the short distance between there and here. It wouldn't pose much of a difficulty to hit the car, or cars, en route, especially as they came through the narrow canyon of buildings at the entrance to the village. Or as they crossed the single-lane, basically medieval bridge.

But they wouldn't do that. They would do it here, in front of the hous-ing project, before the assembled crowds and cameras. If they were going to do it at all. They wanted coverage and publicity for whatever cause it was they believed in and were seeking to further.

Two police motor bikes came into view. The vanguard. The bikes stopped, one on each side of the road.

The first car arrived. Jake watched it slow to a halt. Young suits slid out. Royal Protection suits, presumably. They were as unobtrusive and discreet as they could be. They attracted attention for only a moment or two.

The second car stopped. More suits emerged. These were older, bulkier and greyer. Dignitaries. Councillors. Political figures. Community leaders. He couldn't see the Prime Minister amongst them.

Then the third car arrived and the familiar figure appeared. Slightly stooped now. Balding. Smiling that same old self-deprecating smile. Who, me? Is it me you've come to see? Really? How extraordinary! He waved to the watching faithful and made for the steps leading up to the entrance to the housing project, guided by local officialdom's gentle hand.

Jake held his breath, and let it out only when the visitor was out of sight indoors. Nothing! Nothing had happened. Nothing at all.

But it wasn't over. He continued scanning the crowd and the windows opposite, searching for someone or something – anything! – that should-n't be there.

His phone vibrated. He glanced at it. Anna.

'Anything happening?' she asked.

'Not a thing.'

'I've seen Ed.'

'What?'

'Ed Donaldson. He's here. I caught sight of him for a moment. Then I lost him in the crowd.'

Jake thought quickly. So he hadn't imagined the face in the crowd. It wasn't over. Donaldson wouldn't be here if it was. Especially if he was in trouble.

'Keep looking,' he told her. 'But stay well clear if you see him again.'

Then he rang Bob Cunningham. 'Donaldson is around still,' he said without preamble.

'That right? I assumed he would be in London, well out of the way.'

'He's here.'

'You've seen him?'

'I caught a glimpse. Now someone who has had a lot to do with him recently has confirmed it.'

'I'll see what we can do.'

'What's happening?'

Jake looked round. 'Hi, Ced. Nothing's happening. Nothing out of the ordinary. How's Cait?'

'She's fine now, thanks to you and Dixie.'

'Good.'

'You look as though you've got a problem?'

'Well . . . Dixie took out the sniper. He was in Mains House.'

Cedric nodded judiciously. 'A good choice of location.' Then he added, 'She's pretty good, that Dixie, isn't she?'

'The best.'

'So what's the problem?'

'The Prince has got into the building unscathed. I can't figure out why. Donaldson's still around. Anna's seen him.'

'Maybe they plan to hit him on his way out?'

'How are they going to manage that without a sniper?'

Cedric nodded, conceding the point. 'What about the PM? Is he here?'

'Not yet. He's running late.'

Cedric adjusted his glasses and looked at somewhere very distant. Jake turned back to the window.

'Maybe you got it wrong, Jake,' Cedric said a moment later.

'Probably. I get most things wrong.'

'Maybe we all did.'

The crowd was remarkably calm and still, patient and good-humoured. People were enjoying the occasion. You could tell. Especially the little kids. Big day out. Whatever it was about, it beat going to school.

'They would have had a back-up plan,' Cedric said patiently.

'What?'

'More than one sniper, possibly.'

'If they did, he was probably one of them we got at Kirknewton.'

Jake wasn't really listening. He was still concentrating on what was going on outside.

'Or some other option,' Cedric droned on. 'They wouldn't just give up, not when they've gone to all this trouble and sacrificed so many men.'

'You're talking cock, Ced! They've got no-one left.'

'There's Donaldson still. You said you've seen him. What's he up to?'

Jake didn't respond. That worried him, too, especially since Anna's phone call.

'He's got nobody left, Ced. He has to be here himself.'

Cedric shook his head. 'Maybe you got it wrong, Jake.'

Jake turned towards him in exasperation. But the question he had in mind died still-born when he saw Cedric's face. 'What?' he asked instead, urgently. 'What are you thinking?'

'Maybe the Prince never was the target. Have you thought of that possibility?'

Jake's mind went into rapid reverse. Wheels span as he retraced his thoughts. 'The Prime Minister?' he said quietly.

Cedric nodded. 'Perhaps,' he said.

CHAPTER FORTY-TWO

He was in the wrong place! The realization came like a kick between the legs. For a moment he felt winded. His head was spinning out of control. He was paralysed.

'Jake?'

He looked round blankly at Cedric. Then he grimaced and nodded. 'I hope you're wrong, Ced, but I don't think you are.'

He couldn't reach Bob Cunningham. There was no answer. He didn't leave a message. He moved on.

'Anna, which way will MacGregor come in?'

'MacGregor?'

'He's not here yet, and I think he's the real target.'

'The Prime Minister? Are you sure?'

'No, of course I'm not bloody sure! Sorry. I take that back. And I hope I'm wrong. Which way? Cunningham said they were providing a fast escort.'

'He'll be coming from the north. From his constituency office in Berwick.'

He called Dixie. Within a couple of minutes she joined him at the garage where he kept the car. He already had the BMW started and ready to go.

'Where will it be?' Jake asked as Dixie pored over the map.

'At the edge of the forest, probably.'

'That's what I thought. There's a back way over the moor we can use. Let's hope we can get there in time.'

*

It was a good set-up. From their position higher up, they watched Morgan's people – two men, doing their last-minute checks.

'The very latest in insurgent technology,' Jake murmured. 'The roadside bomb. It rarely fails.'

'Two of them,' Dixie pointed out. 'If the first doesn't get you, the second one will.'

They were fifty yards apart, the two bombs. And they were located where the road became a steep descent into the village, the point at which the official cars would be slowing down.

More certain than bullets, Jake thought. Even a heavily armoured car wouldn't necessarily withstand the blast. 'He learned a thing or two in his years overseas,' he said.

Dixie nodded. 'He's not here himself, is he?'

'Can't see him.'

'He doesn't need to be, I guess. So how do you want to play this, Jake?'

'Take out the bombers before the car appears.'

'I can do that.'

'There're two of them.'

'You need to be back in Cragley, Jake.'

He nodded. She was right. This wouldn't be the only battlefield.

Dixie slipped away. He watched her disappear into the undergrowth. Then he turned to jog back to the car.

His phone vibrated just as he reached the car. Cunningham.

'What have you got for me, Jake?'

'Roadside bombs. Two of them on the road in from the north at the edge of the forest. And two men waiting to detonate them. You'd better divert the Prime Minister, or stop him. He's the real target, not the Prince.'

'MacGregor? You sure?'

'I am now.'

He gave a precise location for the bombs. Then he rang Dixie and told her to hold off. Watching brief only.

'Cavalry coming?' she asked.

'I hope so. We've got to leave them with something to do.'

Then he got in the car and headed back to the village. The job wasn't finished yet. He had Will Rogers to find. He still couldn't think of him as Ed Donaldson. But whatever name he bore, he was the same man. And this was pay-back time for Ellie. This was the day he'd thought would never come.

Things were proceeding to plan back in the village, despite the Prime Minister's unlamented failure to appear on time. Jake glanced at his watch. Soon the visitors would be emerging from the new housing complex, their duty done. No sign of Donaldson. Maybe he had slunk away. Maybe he was keeping his powder dry until the PM appeared. Jake decided to see if Anna was back at the house.

She wasn't. He found Cedric and Caitlin sitting by the window of their living room, gazing wearily over the crowds below. A lot had been happening in their lives. They were entitled to be weary.

Cedric looked round. 'Problems?'

Jake shook his head. 'The PM is being diverted, or stopped.'

Cedric nodded.

'Who would want his job?' Caitlin asked. 'Living like that all the time. We expect too much of our politicians. It's worse than being manager of the England football team.'

Jake thought it a reasonable point. 'How are you feeling, Cait?' he asked.

'I'm fine, thank you.' She gave him a mischievous smile. 'Did I dream it, or did you really carry me out of a house and away in your arms, Jake?'

Thankfully, his phone rang to spare him more embarrassment. It was Anna.

'The Prime Minister's just arrived, Jake.'

He grimaced. 'So he's not been stopped?'

'Can't have been. He's just gone into the housing complex the back way. Joining up with the main party even if he is late. What do you want me to do?'

He cursed silently. The bloody man! Obviously, Cunningham had only been able to divert him, not stop him. The lure of the cameras had been too much to forgo. Bloody politicians!

'Come back to the house, Anna. Meet up here.'

Cedric glanced at him as he ended the call.

'Anna. She says MacGregor has managed to get here after all. Damned idiot!'

Cedric nodded. 'Nothing more you can do, Jake. You've done your bit. More than enough.'

Jake was reluctant to accept that but he couldn't think of anything more he could do. He stood staring through the window at the crowds below for a moment. Then he rang Cunningham.

'What happened?'

'We managed to divert him but he wouldn't turn back.'

'So I gather.'

'Armed colleagues have cordoned off the bombs and picked up the men with them.'

'Alive?'

'Surprisingly, yes. Some woman had tied them up. So they said.'

'Get away!' Jake said, feeling relieved.

'Amazing, isn't it?'

'Absolutely.'

'You and I should get together sometime and see if we can work out how that happened.'

'I'd like that, Bob.'

'Me, too. Got to go now. No sign of Donaldson yet, but we're still looking.'

'Good luck.'

It was as he was closing down his phone that he heard a commotion on the stairs. He frowned and turned towards the door.

The door burst open. Anna was propelled into the room. Behind her came the face Jake had never forgotten. A Hech-Kochler pistol switched from Anna to Jake.

'I tried to stop him!' Anna blurted out tearfully. She was shaking with terror. Her face was convulsed, her body falling apart. Floods of tears were imminent.

Jake nodded and stood still. 'Will Rogers,' he said calmly, 'not Ed Donaldson at all.'

'My instincts were right,' Rogers said, looking hard at Jake. 'You've caused a lot of trouble. Pity we didn't take you out, as well as Sanderson.'

'Doug Kennedy,' Jake said. 'That's how I remember him.'

'What's in a name?' Rogers gave a harsh little laugh. 'It doesn't matter now anyway.'

There was a question Jake just had to ask. He had waited far too long for an answer.

'What happened to Ellie?'

'I knew that would still be bothering you. I shot her,' Rogers said calmly. 'OK? She refused my order. Said it was unreasonable and unlawful. In a country like that!' He shook his head in mock astonishment. 'Battlefield conditions, Jake. I was entitled to shoot her.'

Jake controlled himself and managed not to say anything. He studied his options, considering when and how to go for the gun. Or whether to draw his own weapon. The killing time was near. One or other of them would not leave the room alive.

'Things have gone a bit astray here,' Rogers said conversationally. 'So I'm doing some tidying up myself.'

'Now Jake,' Anna said equally conversationally, straightening up and grabbing Rogers's gun arm. She used both her own arms to force the gun to point towards the ceiling.

Jake recovered from his surprise fast. He stepped forward and delivered a massive blow that floored Rogers. As he went down there was a distinct crack as a bone in the arm Anna was holding gave way. Jake hit him again to make sure. Then he stood back to let Anna take the gun away.

'Great performance!' he said admiringly.

'I had you fooled, didn't I?'

'Why no!'

'I'm too late, am I?'

Jake glanced round at Dixie, who had appeared in the doorway. 'Not by much,' he said.

Dixie walked into the room. 'Are you going to do it,' she said, producing her gun, 'or do I get the pleasure?'

Even as he studied the stricken and dazed figure on the floor, Jake felt the urge fading. He heard Dixie clear the mechanism on her weapon. He knew she was ready, even if he wasn't. Still he hesitated.

'I have a better idea,' another voice said.

Now Bob Cunningham had appeared in the doorway. Jake reached out a restraining hand to Dixie. She looked into his eyes, her gun pointing at Rogers, still ready to do it. He shook his head. She held his gaze for a moment longer. Then she shrugged and stepped away, fading into the background.

'Stand aside, please,' Cunningham said, bustling into the room, followed by a trio of heavily armed colleagues. 'We've been looking for this gentleman. I'm very pleased you've found him for us.'

When next Jake looked round, he noticed that Dixie was no longer in the room. He looked at Anna questioningly. She shrugged. Gone! she mouthed.

Same old Dixie, he thought with a feeling of relief. It would have done none of them any good, least of all her, if she'd stayed. He was grateful for Bob Cunningham's blind eye.

CHAPTER FORTY-THREE

'Don't tell me,' Bob Cunningham said. 'Tell me nothing. It will be better for both of us if I don't know.'

'Don't know what?'

'Anything. I don't want to know who she is, or was. I don't want to know what she did, or didn't do. I may need to know a bit more about what you did, Jake. But, if I do, I'll ask. OK?'

Jake kept a straight face and said, 'OK. Come in, Bob.'

'This is Mr and Mrs Turner's house, isn't it?'

'That's right. I'm a guest. But Cedric won't mind us using his study.'

'He's an old colleague, I understand?'

Jake nodded. 'So it seems. But I didn't know that when all this started. I didn't know Sanderson – or Doug Kennedy, as he used to be – was living in the area either.'

'You spooks!' Bob Cunningham said with a grin.

'Ex-spooks.'

'If you say so.'

'I do – very definitely.'

'Thank the Lord I'm just an old-fashioned copper.'

Jake grinned and motioned to him to sit down. 'So what's the state of play?'

'Donaldson has been handed over to the boys from the Met. There's a higher jurisdiction wants to deal with him. I can't say I'm sorry either. We've got a lot on at the moment.'

'Oh?'

'Sheep rustling up the Ingram Valley, amongst other things. Shoplifting in Amble. My Chief Constable doesn't want his precious resources diverted too long on this unfortunate business here.'

'I bet he doesn't. So what happens now?

'Donaldson? Maybe they'll shoot him? You tell me. I don't know how MI5 operates.'

'I'm pretty sure they won't, although the temptation will be strong. He's caused a lot of death and destruction.'

'In that case, the Crown Prosecution Service will be invited to prepare a case against him. In the end I would imagine he'll spend most of the rest of his life behind bars.'

Jake wondered if that was good enough. It would have been a damned sight more satisfying to have let Dixie go ahead and shoot the bastard.

'It wouldn't have worked,' Bob Cunningham said quietly, understanding what he was thinking. 'I would have had to arrest you then, and anyone with you, and you would have been the people facing trial. It couldn't have been avoided.'

It could, though, Jake thought wistfully. Dixie could have shot you, as well! He sighed. But Cunningham was right. He knew that. There would never have been an end to it.

'How come you arrived when you did, Bob?'

'Your other lady – the one we know about officially – called us. She'd seen Donaldson coming here. I guess she threw herself into the mix to give us a vital few extra minutes. She did well.'

Jake smiled. Good for Anna! He'd guessed it had been something like that. 'He caught us cold, Bob, coming after us like that. I hadn't expected it.'

'Well, his men were down. It was the last throw of the dice for him. He was coming to clear you all away. Then he was going for the PM. He thought he still might get away with it.'

'He's told you?'

Cunningham nodded.

'Is it too much to hope he told you what it was all about?'

'He was in a talkative mood. The adrenaline was flowing and he wanted to impress us. You were right. He was going for the Prime Minister, who he hates. But he was going to take out the Prince as well.'

'Why?'

'To cover his tracks. He wanted the Prime Minister's death to look like an accident. He was to appear an innocent bystander so as to sow confusion. Donaldson wanted to set back the Scottish independence movement without seeming to do so.'

'Because appearing to stifle it would actually have helped it?' Jake murmured.

Cunningham nodded. 'At the first sign of interference from the Security Service the Nationalists would have declared immediate independence.'

'And he thought his solution would work? Assassinating the Prince?'

'Apparently. There would have been a tide of sympathy for the Crown and the Union from one end of the country to the other.'

'MacGregor supports the Union, though, doesn't he?'

'He says so.'

'But Donaldson thought he knew different?'

Cunningham nodded again. 'So it appears.'

Jake thought it over and then pronounced what to him was the only conclusion any sane person could reach. 'The man's mad!'

Cunningham didn't disagree. 'There're a few of them around, unfortunately. Madmen. More than ever, in fact. The world's not what it was when I joined the Force.'

Jake shook his head. It was such a banal end, and there'd been so much violence to reach it. No sense to it at all.

Bob Cunningham looked up and smiled. 'Anyway, Jake, what are your plans? Are you stopping here?'

'In Cragley? I don't know. If I did, I'd have to rebuild my cottage. But I'm not sure it would be worth it.'

'Well, let me know if you decide to do that. I'll give you a hand. In a year or two's time – maybe less – I'm going to be a man of leisure. I'll be desperate for something to spend my spare time on. Helping you rebuild your cottage would be just the job.'

'Thanks, Bob. Pensioner, eh? I'll bear that in mind. Have you any skills?'

'I've done a course in dry stone walling at the tech college. How's that?'

'It's a start.'

The other man nodded. 'That's right. Now, I suppose, I'd better go and have a word with the Turners. See how they are.'

Jake got up to escort him to The Gallery, where Cedric and Caitlin had gone to seek and reclaim normality. 'I'll come with you to collect my cat,' he said.

Rebuild the cottage? It was a thought. But he didn't know if he could do that. He didn't know if he wanted to stay here, in a crazy place like this, now Ellie had been put to rest at last. Now he'd got justice for her, justice of a kind.

Maybe he should just get up and go? He could have a look at Uncle Bob's old place in North Yorkshire. Claim his inheritance, which he hadn't seen since he was a lad. Or, possibly better yet, just go somewhere totally new and start afresh.

He collected Apache, who seemed ready to leave and go home now he'd cleaned out the local mice, and headed out to find the Land Rover. He wanted to have a look at what was left of his cottage before he took any actual decisions. Besides, he still had things to do here, issues to resolve, hopes to cling to, and not everything depended on himself alone.

He could see he wasn't the only one who had wanted to see what was left of the cottage. Long before he got there, he noticed fresh tyre treads in the mud at the edge of puddles on the track. It might have been Bob Cunningham's people, or his friends from the south, but he didn't think so. He had a pretty good hunch who it was.

He parked next to a small 4-wheel-drive Suzuki in his usual parking place. Apache, having looked out of the window, showed no inclination to get out.

For a moment Jake surveyed the desolate scene and pictured how it had been, and how it still might be again. Then he thought of the derelict farmsteads all over the hills of the county and wondered if this was destined to be another abandoned ruin.

'Thought I'd find you here,' he called, getting out of the Land Rover.

She nodded and raised a hand in greeting. He walked over to where she was sitting on the wall.

'Come to say good-bye?' he asked.

She nodded again. Then she stopped smiling. 'You should have let me take him, Jake,' she said bitterly.

'It wouldn't have done us much good, Dixie. We would have been looking at years of criminal trials – with us the defendants, not him. Years of being remanded in custody, and then years of prison, probably.'

She thought it over and eventually found a way to accept that. 'Well, we fixed him good, I guess. We've paid him back for Ellie. He's still got a life, but it's not much of a one. So bad, in fact, he might choose to opt out of it.'

'True. You did well, Dixie. I can't tell you how much I appreciate it.'

'*We* did well, Jake.' She gave him a sunny smile. 'Like old times, eh? Me and you? Against the odds?'

'Just a little bit!' He laughed and shook his head. 'Where to now, Dixie?'

'Don't ask, Jake. Just give me a call when you've decided what you're going to do. Let me know.'

'You don't think I'll just carry on here? Rebuild my house and get back to where I was?'

She shook her head. 'Not really. Do you?'

'I don't know yet. I really don't.'

'You will, Jake. You'll know eventually what's right for you. Take care. Be good to yourself – and don't spend your time looking back.'

'And you take care, Dix. You, too.'

She stood up. They hugged one another. Then she left. He didn't watch. And she didn't look back. She never looked back. He wasn't sure he could live like that. He waited until the Suzuki was out of sight before he returned to the Land Rover, and to Apache.

There was still someone else to see. And he needed to see her most of all.

She came back to Cedric's place late at night, worn out, and carrying a big parcel wrapped in polythene. 'Thought I'd find you here,' she said with a big smile.

'I might have left. Ever think of that possibility?'

'No. Never.' She shook her head with utter certainty.

'What's in the parcel?'

'It's your dragonfly painting,' she said, beginning to extricate it from the wrappings.

'How. . . ?'

'I wasn't going to let that go – even if you were!'

He stared at the painting and shook his head with amazement. 'Thank you,' he said, touched by the effort she had made. 'It will be good to have something from the old place.'

She smiled. 'You're very welcome.'

'Something else,' she said. 'I've been making my peace. My boss says I'm off the hook. I'll be OK.'

'That's good.'

'I knew you would wait for me,' she added, as if he had only just asked her the question.

He smiled and said, 'So what happens now?'

'I've been thinking it over.'

'And?'

He held his breath.

She held up two airline tickets. 'I've bought us a holiday in Corfu. I thought that would give us time to work something out and make plans.'

'Perfect,' he murmured as Anna came to be kissed. 'Just perfect.'